Stink Alley

To the terrific readers at the School Library—

Jamie Gilson

Dec. 3, 2002

Stink Alley

By Jamie Gilson

HarperCollinsPublishers

Library of Congress Cataloging-in-Publication Data
Gilson, Jamie.
    Stink alley / by Jamie Gilson.
        p.   cm.
    Summary: Living in Holland in 1614 with the harsh Puritan leader, William Brewster, and
working for the family of a mischievous Dutch boy named Rembrandt, a spirited twelve-year-old
orphan girl struggles to do what is right.
    ISBN 0-688-17864-2 — ISBN 0-06-029217-2 (library binding)
    [1. Puritans—Fiction.   2. Christian life—Fiction.   3. Cooks—Fiction.   4. Artists—Fiction.
5. Netherlands—History—17th century—Fiction.]   Title.
PZ7.G4385 Su   2002   2001039515
[Fic]—dc21   CIP
                                                                                 AC

Typography by Henrietta Stern
1   2   3   4   5   6   7   8   9   10
❖
First Edition

Acknowledgments

My thanks to Dr. Jeremy Dupertuis Bangs, director of the Leiden American Pilgrim Museum. I appreciate his gracious welcome to me in Leiden and his willingness to share his encompassing knowledge about the Pilgrims and their lives. Johanna Young, now of the Isle of Man, made the swaddling baby doll I bought in the 1970s in the Leiden Pilgrim Documents Center and named Hannah in my story. She took me to Stink Alley (now officially named William Brewster Steeg) and told me about wooden shoe boats and clattering hoops in the streets. None of the mistakes that I made in writing *Stink Alley* is the fault of these kind advisors.

Central to the story was William Bradford's *Of Plymouth Plantation 1620–1647*, edited by Samuel Eliot Morison (New York: Alfred A. Knopf, 1952). Also especially helpful were *Pilgrim Life in Leiden* by Jeremy Dupertuis Bangs (1997); *Daily Life in Rembrandt's Holland* by Paul Zumthor (Stanford, Calif.: Stanford University Press, 1994); *Daily Life in Holland in the Year 1566* by Rien Poortvliet (New York: Harry N. Abrams, 1992); *Rembrandt* by Gary Schwartz (New York: Harry N. Abrams, 1992); *Rembrandt and Seventeenth-Century Holland* by Claudio Pescio (New York: Peter Bedrick Books, 1995); *The English Housewife* by Gervase Markham (1615); *The Dutch Table* by Gillian Riley (San Francisco: Pomegranate Artbooks, 1994); and *The History of Underclothes* by C. Willet and Phillis Cunnington (New York: Dover Publications, 1992).

The book would not have been written at all without the encouragement and insightful suggestions of my editors, Susan Pearson and Melanie Donovan. I am grateful to them and to my always wise and patient husband, Jerry.

For

    Samuel James Gilson
    Noah Edward Gilson
    Griffin William LaLonde
    and
    Tess Marie LaLonde

Pilgrims in the New World

Chapter One

"**I** HEARD HIM, LIZZY," Clara said. "He screamed all the way down." She cracked an egg into a big bowl of flour and butter. '*Aieeeeeeeeee!*' Like that. Only louder. It curdled your blood." She cracked another egg. "The alarm bell woke me. It must have woke you. Even as far as Stink Alley."

Lizzy had only heard the news that morning. On the way to work, she'd passed clusters of people telling the story. "*Aieeeeeeeeeee!*" an old man had cried. "Like that! Broke every bone in his body." "*Aieeeeeeeeeee!*" a young woman had told her friends. "And that, I warned my boys, is why you stay well away from windmills."

In the night, they all said, lightning had struck one of Leiden's windmills. A big one. Men had come running

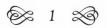 1

with their leather buckets and ladders. It was a watchman, they said, who'd screamed. He'd got too close. One of the windmill's long arms had snagged him, whirled him all the way around, and then dashed him to the ground. The wrath of God, some people said, "*Aieeeeeeeeeee!*"

A predawn rain had washed most of the smoke from the air, and the early September morning was clear and warm. It was already eight o'clock, but Lizzy Tinker had been at work since daylight, helping out in the Van Heusdens' kitchen.

Lizzy pulled a squirming gray eel out of a tub of warm water. The eel was as long as her arm. "God rest the good man's soul," she told Clara, the Van Heusdens' cook. With the back of her hand, Lizzy wiped a stray black curl out of her eye. Then she pressed the eel firmly on a slippery board and, with a hammer blow smartly to its head, knocked it dead.

A child's yellow wooden shoe was floating in the tub. The tail of a second eel slapped it.

"Stop that, you wretched sea monster!" ordered a boy who was the shoe's captain. He twirled the shoe around the tub one more time, then scooped up a red-and-white pinwheel from the wet kitchen floor. "I'm going outside," he announced, gathering up his long green skirt and petticoat. "Don't let them sink my ship, sailor!"

Lizzy was twice as old as the boy, but small. His skirt and

apron would almost fit her. "Aye, aye, sir," she said.

He dashed out to the cobblestone street, waving the pinwheel. It was an early present for his breeching, to keep him busy till the afternoon celebration began. He was six years old. Today he would give up his babies' skirts to wear the breeches of a big boy. There would be a party with mounds of food.

Lizzy was chopping eel for the party stew. The thought of it made her mouth water. She slit the eel's skin, peeled it off, scooped out the guts, and tossed them into a bucket. Then with her slim, sharp knife, she began to slice the eel's white belly.

"Girl!" Clara put one hand on her broad hip, raised her wooden spoon from the dough she was mixing, and rapped Lizzy's knuckles with a sticky smack. "Are you totally empty of wit? Look at the size of those eel chunks. I told you, chop it fine so it'll go far. And toss more onions in the pot. We've got twenty hungry mouths to feed tonight. Young Jacob loves eel. He'll be dripping it all over his fine new taffeta coat." She shook her head fondly.

Lizzy smiled. "I like big fat bites of eel in my stew," she said. "Then you can feel them squoosh in your mouth."

"Well, it's not your stew, is it?" Clara told her sharply, and went back to mashing water and eggs into flour and butter.

 3

"Sorry. I misspoke," Lizzy murmured, cutting the eel into smaller pieces.

"Nay, then, Lizzy, don't fret," Clara went on, smiling. "Most days, I like fat bites, too."

Lizzy glanced at the cook, who was blond and plump— young, too, eighteen, maybe. She was singing now as she pounded away at the pastry dough. "Dum, de dum doooo."

"I hope you don't mind my saying this," Lizzy told her. Clara stopped singing and looked up with narrowed eyes. "That crust you're making," Lizzy went on, "for the cherry tart. You need a lighter touch. It's going to turn out tough if you work it so eager like."

"Well, I do mind, don't I. I don't ask advice of an English runt," Clara told her, kneading the dough harder. "I've got advice for *you*. Good kitchen help knows when to keep its mouth shut."

Lizzy bit her lip. She did talk too much. Master Brewster said so. Often. He was a wise man, so what he said must be true.

Lizzy lived with the Brewster family, had for almost a month now, ever since her dear papa died. Papa had called her his joy. How she missed him.

It was all of six years ago, in 1608, that she and Papa and Sally, her stepmother, had left Scrooby, England, with William Brewster. More than fifty villagers had fled with him to Holland, breaking the law to do it. The law said they had to go to the king's church, and they'd refused to. So they'd broken one law by separating themselves from the Church of England and another by leaving the country without the king's permission. They were Separatists. They could have been killed for it.

Once they got to Holland, they were safe, but life was hard. Then this year, it had gotten awful. First Sally died, then Papa. Leiden could have put her in its orphanage, but the Brewsters had taken her in. They gave her space to sleep and food to eat. And Lizzy was grateful. Orphans lived behind barred windows. A girl without parents, she'd learned, had to be careful.

"Ahoy, sailor," a small voice called from the kitchen door, "did you let the wretched sea monsters sink my ship?"

"Not a chance, Captain," Lizzy told him. "It's still afloat on the high seas, and the last wretched sea monster is about to meet its fate." She gave the boy a fast salute and pulled the final eel high out of the water so he could see it wiggle. He shrieked and ran.

Lizzy had floated wooden shoe boats herself. Though she and Papa and Sally went always to Meeting with the other Scrooby families, they'd lived well apart from them, out behind the blacksmith's shop, where her father had worked at the forge. They'd been friends with their Dutch neighbors, and Lizzy had often played street games with Dutch children until dusk.

Now she was the Brewsters' guest. But she wouldn't be a leech. She would pay for her keep. Work wasn't easy to find. Sally had taught her to cook and bake, but those were common skills. Once she found a job, it would be harder to hold on to than the wet eel struggling in her hands.

Lizzy banged the eel on its head and glanced at Clara.

She hadn't meant to annoy her. She'd just wanted to let Clara know she was a good cook.

Lizzy slit the skin and peeled it.

If only she could work here for good, not just this one busy day.

She drew out the guts and began to chop the eel fine.

"Lizzy," Clara said, "first you grate a knob of ginger the size of your thumb into that stew; then you take my biggest basket and hie yourself over to the Blaeus' bakery, down by the Eel Market. I've ordered three braided loaves, ten husks, and two dozen letter cookies. They'll be extra fancy J's for Jacob. And hurry. There's a lot more work to be done."

Lizzy gloried at the thought of a walk on this fine day, but she kept her pleasure hidden so Clara wouldn't see. Quickly, she scraped the rest of the eel into the copper kettle, chopped a few more onions, and grated in the pungent ginger.

"Back in a trice," she told Clara. She pulled tight the ties of the white linen cap that bound her unruly braids, and picking up the market basket, she set off.

Chapter Two

A BIG METAL HOOP rolled toward Lizzy as she stepped out the doorway. Clattering across the cobblestones, the hoop caught the edge of her skirt. That changed its path, and two shouting children dashed away to catch it before it splashed into the canal. The tall gabled house where Lizzy had been working sat close to the water on a canal shaded with linden trees. Over hundreds of years, the city of Leiden had grown, stretching over a cluster of islands crisscrossed by canals and rivers, connected here and there by bridges.

Lizzy headed to the nearest one. Before starting over, she knelt by the canal, put down her basket, flicked a fish head aside, and washed her hands in the calm brown water. She'd get the eel slime out from between her fingers before she picked up the bread. But she'd best be quick. Clara needed her on this party day, but she didn't want help every day. Lizzy had asked, though, if Clara would give a kind word about her to a cook who did need someone.

She stood up, waving her hands in the air to dry. As she did, she spotted a tall, lanky boy in the crowd crossing the bridge ahead. He was holding the sides of his brown cap as if it might blow away, though there was no wind.

"Will!" she called, but he didn't turn. "Will Farley! Will!"

She ran to catch up, swinging the basket. "Will, wait!" Before she reached him, even through lingering smoke, she could smell him. Lizzy had to remind herself not to care. He'd been her friend since they were babies. Now he was a fuller's helper—one of the thousands in Leiden who helped make textiles. All he did every daylight hour— except, of course, on the Lord's Day—was tread barefoot in a wooden tub of water where freshly dyed cloth was steeping. The cloth stank. Urine had been used to set the dye. As Will walked on the woolen cloth, it got softer and stronger and cleaner, but the stink of it clung to his skin.

When she reached him, he was leaning on the bridge rail.

"Why aren't you at work?" she asked, tugging on his doublet. "What's wrong?" When he turned to her, she

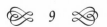

caught her breath. His face was as pale as wheat flour and the whites of his eyes were webbed with red. His thin brown hair stuck to his wet forehead.

"Oh, Lizzy-bit, I threw up again, over and over. Pa and John are still working the wool," he told her, "but I couldn't stay any longer. I'll get no money for the day and they'll mark it up against me." He lowered his head.

Will's family were Separatists from Scrooby, too. Will was twelve, his brother, John, fourteen. They lived with their parents in the newer, cheaper part of town. They lived in one small room, without even a garden. In Scrooby, they'd plowed and planted acres and acres of land around the manor house. Holland was land-poor. It didn't need foreign farmers.

That's the way it was, and Lizzy couldn't change it. She could only try to cheer him. "Come with me," she said. "I'm going to the bakery."

Will's brown woolen breeches and gray doublet looked as faded as he did. He lowered his head, shrugged his shoulders, and followed.

"Take a deep breath," she told him when they passed a saddler's shop. "Smell that sweet tanned leather."

"Makes me think of home," said Will. Even after six years in Holland, home to Will meant Scrooby.

Lizzy poked him with her elbow. "Come on, at least you've got a steady job." They made their way through a crowd of women with shopping baskets to fill. "Mine's just for one day. I'm a very good cook. I am, truly." She knew she was babbling. Maybe it would lighten his sickness. "This morning, I told Clara she was overworking her pastry, and I was dead right about it, but she snapped at me. What do you think—is it still prideful if what you say is true? Papa always said to rein in my pride. But Master Brewster says to crush it. He had me learn a verse from Proverbs last night. Starts out 'When pride cometh, then cometh shame.' I try to remember, I do. Master Brewster says my papa let me be much too free. Master Brewster says Papa was letting me turn Dutch. Master Brewster says . . ."

"'Master Brewster says. Master Brewster says.'" Will stopped and leaned close to her face. "So, once he was master of Scrooby Manor. So what! He doesn't know all!" Lizzy stepped back from the force of Will's fury. His face was no longer white. It was crimson. And a vein in his temple throbbed. "He doesn't. That's what I think. All day long in the fulling tubs, I think, nothing else to do with my head. All day, I lift my feet up and mash them down, and knead the foul fabric with my toes so my legs don't cramp. I watch Pa try to do it in the next tub over. But he needs a field to plow. He followed William Brewster here, but he doesn't belong." Will's voice grew tight. "God is in England, too."

Lizzy was stunned. Nobody spoke ill of Master Brewster.

Nobody *she'd* ever heard. And Master Brewster hated unjust anger. He called it evil. An angry man, he said, was a hideous monster. And Will was *very* angry.

"You know what William Brewster thinks?" he went on. "He fancies he's Moses, brought us out of bondage into the Promised Land. Well, he isn't. He shouldn't have led us here. That's what *I* think. I think he doesn't know all about you or God or my pa or anything else."

He had started to cry, his shoulders heaving. To keep her from seeing, he turned and ran, without a wave good-bye.

She watched him go. It so took her breath away that she couldn't even call him back. Such awful things he'd said. He was wrong. Lizzy was certain. Her papa had always said that Master Brewster knew what was best. Master Brewster was educated. Master Brewster had gone to the university at Cambridge, and when he read the Bible, he knew what God meant by it. He didn't need the English bishops to tell him. None of them, he said, needed the bishops telling them what to think. That's why they'd left.

Deep in thought, Lizzy kept walking. When she looked up, she was already at the Blaeus' bakery. It had been a while since she'd been there, since well before her father died. Sally had helped out at the bakery several times, making spicy meat pies and sweet Banbury cakes for big banquets. Sally had said it was the best place in Leiden for fine cookies and light buttery pancakes.

Catharina Blaeu, the baker's wife, was standing next to the pretzel rack, one hand resting on her huge belly. She was dealing with a press of customers, all in a hurry.

"Will the baby come soon?" Lizzy asked when she'd placed her order. "It looks to be a sturdy size."

"Anytime now, I hope," Catharina said, packing the bread and cookies in Lizzy's basket. "I've been suffering. Flat on my back the most of these last weeks. The midwife says it may be twins. Girls, I hope. To help with the cookies." She rested her hand warmly on Lizzy's shoulder. "I was sorry to hear about your father."

"Yes," Lizzy said, "he was abed only a week. We'd tried leeches, and the barber had bled him twice, and I was so hoping—" A woman behind her cleared her throat loudly. "Thank you," Lizzy told Catharina, and turned away with her heaping basket.

"Ho, Lizzy!" The baker's son, Jan, waved from the baking room. He always had a ready word for her. "Birthday party?" He was shirtless in the heat, stoking the fire with wood. No musty peat taste for the Blaeus' bread.

"A breeching at the Van Heusdens'," she called back, smiling. "Little Jacob." Late afternoons, with Sally, she'd often stopped to talk with Jan as he rinsed his oven mop in the murky canal water.

"Happy times, then," he called, and slammed shut the oven door.

Happy times. For some. When was Will last happy? Lizzy wondered. She thought of his angry words all the way back to the fine house on the canal.

Jacob was sitting on the front stoop, his knees open wide. In the cradle of the skirt between his legs lay a small brown-and-white puppy, sleeping soundly. "He's my present," Jacob told her. "They tried to hide him, but I heard him bark and bark. Madam my mother said I could have him before the party if I was a good boy. I'm thinking of names. Can I have a cookie?"

Chapter Three

"*H*URRY HOME, NOW, before it turns dark," Clara said, pressing two coins into Lizzy's hand. "And go tomorrow early to the Gerritzen place. They maybe can use you. Tell the mistress I'll speak for you. You're sassy, but you work hard, I give you that."

Night was not safe in the streets, so Lizzy walked briskly. She'd had a royal supper, rich juices and tiny bits of eel left over from the stew. She'd wiped them out of the almost-empty bowl with a piece of soft white braided bread. The platter of calves' feet with tripe and peas had been scraped clean. Every crumb of the golden brown cookies was gone, but not, Lizzy noted, the tough-crusted cherry tart.

As she crossed the bridge, she could hear the guests still singing and the fiddler playing a merry tune.

By the time she reached the Brewsters' house, it was dusk. They lived down a dark passage, around the corner from St. Peter's Church. It was so narrow that when she reached out her arms, she could almost touch the red-brick buildings on either side. It was called Stink Alley. If you wondered how it got its name, all you had to do was breathe in.

The top half of the Brewsters' door was open, and light from the lamps inside still flickered. They hadn't left for Thursday-night Meeting. Good. Still, Lizzy was late. Master Brewster required promptness. He had rules and, as she was their guest, she must obey them.

She walked in with a smile that begged forgiveness, and a short curtsy. "Good evening," she said.

William Brewster was sitting in his folding leather chair near the door. He turned his head and regarded her steadily with deep-set ice blue eyes. "You are late, Elizabeth," he said evenly. His short gray hair and goatee were sharply cut, so that his face seemed all edges. "You have interrupted our prayer." He lowered his head, rubbed his eyes with his thumb and forefinger, and closed the Bible in his lap.

The whole family stared at her. Except Love. Love, almost four years old, sat on the floor, inspecting a scab on his knee through a new hole in his stocking. At Meetings, it was Love who, twitching about, most often felt the switch of the birch rod. His mother, Mary, was rocking the baby, Wrestling, in his cradle. When she looked at Lizzy, her lips tightened. Fourteen-year-old Patience, whose lips pursed like her mother's, stopped her knitting and sat up straight on the long, backless bench. Fear, who was eight, stood pressed against the sideboard, her hands clasped behind her.

The silence that went with their stares made the hairs on Lizzy's neck prickle. She tried to explain. "The job I told you of," she began, "it lasted long. It was a special party for a little boy's breeching and there were dishes to do, some of them silver. And the kitchen floor wanted two scrubbings. I was needed." She waited. William Brewster frowned.

The Brewsters were good to take her in, truly, Lizzy thought, but it wasn't easy to please them. Her papa would have asked her questions about the day. The Brewsters asked none.

"I got paid." She gave Mistress Brewster the coins. "And the cook there, she told me of a place they might be wanting a kitchen helper full-time. She said I was a good worker and she'd put in a word."

A shiny brass platter on the fireplace mantel caught the light from a candle in front of it. From the glow it cast, she could see Master Brewster's frown deepen.

Was what I said prideful? Lizzy wondered. I must say

something now that's not about me. It had been such a fine party. She could tell them.

"The boy's name was Jacob. He got a green taffeta coat and shiny new breeches, and he ran into the kitchen all dressed up to show us what a big boy he was. Everybody gave him such hugs and kisses, and he got presents—a red-and-white pinwheel, a set of knucklebones, and a puppy dog he named Arf."

Love stood up. "I want a dog," he said. "I want a pinwheel, too. I want it yellow."

"Elizabeth! Stop at once!" Master Brewster said sharply. "Do you see what effect you've had? You are like the serpent that tempted the wife of Adam." He turned away.

"Love," he said sternly, "come here." Love's bottom lip quivered. He stepped forward. "You are not to say 'I want.' All that you require, you are provided with. You are to be ever thankful for what you have. You must take your good sister Fear as your model." He rested his hand on her shoulder. "She is perfectly obedient."

Master Brewster turned back to Lizzy and frowned. "Elizabeth, shame," he said, lowering his voice. "Shame. Your words corrupt my children. Love is still a young twig, easily bent toward evil." He paused, looking at Love steadily until Love, glancing first at Fear, lowered his eyes. "Children are not to be so coddled. That behavior is disgusting."

"Yes, Master Brewster," Lizzy said, but she wanted to explain. "They had prayers at the party, too—I could hear—and it just seemed like such a happy time, I—"

"Elizabeth, enough!" Master Brewster told her. "Tie up your loose tongue. Remember that you are a guest in this house. Do not sow discord under my roof. Patience, extinguish the lights. Fear, put the coverfire over the flames. It is time for us to leave for Meeting." He rose from his chair, folded it, and leaned it against the wall.

He started out the doorway, his tall hat almost touching the top. Then he turned back. "Elizabeth." His voice was harsh. "Had you been listening to Pastor Robinson at Meeting, you would know that in all children there is a stubbornness and stoutness of mind. It rises, he explains, from sinful pride, which must be broken and beaten down. He has said that children should not learn that they *have* a will of their own but must learn to do God's will. And his word is the word of truth. While you are in my house, Elizabeth, you will not corrupt my children as your father has corrupted you."

Lizzy could see the disgust in his eyes. She clenched her teeth to keep from speaking. It was true—her mind did wander during the long sermons. I may not be good, she thought, but my papa was. He was a kind man. It stung when Master Brewster spoke ill of him.

Master Brewster stepped out into Stink Alley. Lizzy

stayed back and waited for his family to follow. Love and Fear were the last to go. Fear took a tiny rag doll she'd had clenched in her fist and tucked it into the drawstring bag that hung at her side. During the long Meetings, Lizzie had watched her rest her hand on it, rubbing its soft fabric, thinking far thoughts.

When they had all left, Lizzy laid her cheek against the cool plaster wall and closed her eyes. She was tired. But Thursday was Meeting night. The parsonage, called the Green Close, where they had Meeting, was only a short walk from Stink Alley. Some walked far to get there. Others were just a step away, in a group of small dwellings just behind the parsonage. But from far or near, everyone was expected at Meeting. Lizzy closed the door and moved into the narrow passage of Stink Alley.

Master Brewster thought she was bad. It must be true. God must think so, too. What if girls like her, spoiled by their papas, could never be turned around right?

In front of her, in the dim light, Love was clinging to Fear's skirt. Fear was hugging her shoulders tightly. Lizzy moved closer.

"I saw," Love told Fear. "I saw what you put in your bag. You're not supposed to play with dolls in Meeting." And he began to chant in her ear.

"Satan will get you 'cause you've been bad. Satan will get you. And I'll be glad."

Chapter Four

IN THE NIGHT, Fear had tugged at Lizzy's arm, waking her. "Listen," Fear had whispered. "In the corner. Do you hear? It's Satan."

Lizzy had heard scratching. It was by a barrel of flour stored in the corner. Maybe mice. Maybe not. To make Fear go back to sleep, Lizzy had told her, hoping it was true, that Satan couldn't climb steps on his cloven hooves. But Fear was eight, and she was smart. She thought about things. She'd heard at Meetings that Satan was here in Leiden, dancing in the streets. If he could dance on those cloven hooves, she'd asked, why couldn't he climb steps? "Why not, then, Lizzy?" she'd whispered. "Why not?"

Lizzy's bed was a straw-filled mattress that she shared

with both Fear and Patience. Fear had woken Lizzy two, maybe three times in the night, afraid in the dark. She lived up to her name, Fear did. Patience didn't. Her sister's night crying irked her. But everything, it seemed, irked Patience.

Now Lizzy was awake without Fear's shaking her. The room was still and dark as a pig's belly. It was almost morning, though, time to get up. Lizzy drew her fingers through the tangles of her long black hair. Her braids had come loose in the night. Binding them up again as best she could, she stretched her feet to the floor.

Her eyes were cat green, but that didn't help Lizzy see in the dark. By now, though, she knew the room and everything in it by feel. She found the chamber pot, used it, and felt for her pile of clothes. She rolled on her stockings, tied them with ribbon garters, and wiggled her toes into her stiff leather shoes. They'd been Sally's best. With only a little lamb's wool stuffed in the toes, they fit her fine. And, imagine, she thought, they'd belonged to a grown woman.

After pulling a gray petticoat over her long shirt, she lifted her top skirt down over her head. The nut brown skirt smelled like the eels she'd cleaned the day before. The shirt smelled like Lizzy. It was all she wore of underwear, and night or day she never took it off. Sweeping up her apron and cap, she tiptoed away from the sounds of sleep and went down the steep circular stairs.

Sitting on the bottom step, she pulled the cap tightly over her wobbly braids and sighed. She had to get a job today and keep it. Everyone else had work to do. Patience and Fear helped at home, so Lizzy wasn't needed here. Their big brother, Jonathan, married and living nearby, made ribbons on a small loom. He'd even found a ready market for them back in England.

As she put on her apron, she glanced at the wall bed. Behind its curtain, Master and Mistress Brewster were still asleep. They both slept sitting up in their cramped sleeping cupboard. Baby Wrestling lay just outside their bed in his wicker cradle. Gently, so as not to disturb them, Lizzy lifted the big clay coverfire off the ashes in the fireplace. Luckily, they were still glowing a bit from the night before. It was Lizzy's job to start the morning fire, and making sparks from the flint and steel of the tinderbox was always tricky. She raised a small flame with the bellows, then stacked pieces of peat in a small round tower over it.

Lizzy's stomach growled. In the half-light, she reached into the bread basket that hung from ropes over the table and took out yesterday's black rye. Tearing off a piece, she placed the rest back in the high basket so the rats and mice couldn't get it.

One last thing remained to be done. She took the

wooden honing board down from its wall hook and spit on it. Carefully, patiently, she pressed her small knife back and forth against the tightly grained wet oak just as Sally had taught her to. Yesterday's eels had dulled it. When the knife felt sharp enough against her thumb, she slipped it into a woolen bag at her waist. She was ready.

She let herself out onto Stink Alley. At Choir Alley, she turned right. Passing old St. Peter's Church, she began to walk briskly along the worn cobblestones, crossing bridge after bridge toward the Gerritzen place, where Clara had told her to go.

A line of red brushed the sky as she finished the last bite of her bread. In half an hour or so, the Yarn Market's bell would ring, the signal that it was time for work to begin.

The sun had not quite risen when she arrived at the house, which was set well back from the Rhine River. The night mist still hung low. In the grassy ramparts in front of the house, the sails of two windmills were making slow circles.

Waiting for the work bell to ring, Lizzy sat down on the wall that held back the river and listened to the creak of turning sails. A rooster crowed. Two men hurried down the bumpy street, leading horses with sacks of barley piled high in their carts. The day was beginning. Lizzy sat up tall. She would *get* this job. She would *keep* this job. She lifted her chin and clamped her lips together.

The moment she did, she opened them again to catch her breath. Through the mist, a long-legged monster was striding toward her, dead-on. Satan? Here? Who else could loom so big? Had she been so bad? The monster, whistling through his teeth, kept taking giant steps straight at her. She couldn't move back. There was nothing behind her but the river, so Lizzy jumped to the grass and pressed herself hard against the wall.

The monster stopped whistling and burped loudly. Now that she could see him more clearly, Lizzy stepped away from the wall and smiled. The monster wore a leather doublet with green stockings. A red velvet cap sat on his wiry russet hair. His nose looked like the white bulb of a green onion. The monster was a boy. A small boy at that, but, on his high wooden stilts, he was taller than a man.

He curled his lip at Lizzy in a small sneer, spun about on one spindly leg, hopped off the stilts, and strolled to the nearest windmill. It was the bigger one, as tall as a three-story house, maybe taller. Its four wings, long wooden arms covered in canvas, moved gears inside the mill. The gears turned grindstones. And the stones ground malt for brewing stout Dutch beer.

When the mill's next sail passed in front of him, the boy glanced at Lizzy to be sure she was watching, then reached out and grabbed it. He swung back and forth, knees bent, as the sail began to lift his feet off the ground.

Lizzy was about to tell him to get off of there right now, when suddenly he screamed. "Help! You! Girl!" he called in a shrill, high voice. "Grab the sail. Stop it!"

Why, the child was in true danger. Lizzy ran toward the mill, hands out. The sail was moving briskly now.

"Stop it! It's caught me!" he yelled.

Leaping high, Lizzy held on to the wooden frame. The sail bounced briefly, but it didn't stop rising. As it lifted, the boy, giggling, dropped to the ground, rolled into a somersault, and stood up.

Without his weight, the sail rose with a jerk. "Now *you* jump," the boy called to her, laughing.

Lizzy was rising toward the sky, but her hands were locked. She couldn't jump. Her head told her that if she held on a breath longer, she'd have to go all the way around. And if she did, her heart, beating fast now, would stop at the top. Still, her fingers would not let go.

The boy reached out and pulled at her feet. One of her shoes came off in his hand.

Lizzy's cheeks burned with the thrill of the ride. She was flying.

"You're supposed to jump! Jump or you'll die!" the boy called.

Lizzy swallowed hard, opened her hands, and fell. Her

skirt billowed. Her linen cap blew off with the wind. Arms out wide to stop the blow, she hit the ground.

The boy came running, panic in his eyes. "If you're dead, it's not my fault," he said.

Chapter Five

*L*IZZY LAY STILL. The path under the mill was as hard as bricks and it had sucked the air out of her like the kick of a horse. Her elbow and chin were both bleeding.

"I was just playing a joke on you," the boy told her. "I didn't want to hurt you. I was being funny. You should have jumped when I told you to. It wasn't so far then. You were dumb not to. Somebody might have seen you, and besides, you could have snapped your neck."

"If you didn't want me to do it," Lizzy told him, gasping, "you shouldn't have asked for help."

Lizzy stared up at the wing she'd ridden. By now, it was almost at the top, cutting across the clear sky. If I'd hung on, she thought with a shiver, that's where I'd be right now. She sat up, reached for her cap, and pulled it back on as well as she could. "I did it, though."

"What are you here for, anyway?" the boy asked. "Who are you, and what's your name? I live there." He nodded toward the brick house behind the mills. With a start, Lizzy realized it was the place she hoped to work.

If this cheeky child is telling the truth, she thought, his mother is the mistress of the house. No matter what he'd done, she'd best not sass him. "My name is Elizabeth Tinker. Lizzy. I am here for the job as kitchen helper. Clara, the cook at the place I worked yesterday, the Van Heusdens', said the cook here was getting feeble and needed help. She said she'd put in a word for me."

"I don't think I like you," the boy said. "You didn't jump when I told you to. I'll tell Madam my mother not to hire you. I'll tell her you're a witch who flies on wind-mill wings. Besides, your apron's dirty, your cap's loose, and your chin's bloody."

Lizzy touched her face. It was true. Her chin *was* scraped. Her apron *was* covered with dirt. She *had* swung on the windmill. Worse, now that she thought about it, she'd loved it. She bit her lip. "Nay, then, it was your trick, not mine, that got me in the air. You know very well I'm not a witch." She tugged at the strings on her cap and looked him hard in the eye.

"If Cook had seen you, *she'd* have called you a witch.

She sees witches everywhere. She told me that when she was a little girl, she knew a farmer who had two pigs die because a witch cast a spell on them." The boy climbed on the river wall and laid her shoe beside him. Then he took a piece of paper from his pocket, set it on the wall, and began to make marks on it with a piece of sharp black chalk. "They tied the witch's thumbs to her big toes and threw her in a canal. She didn't float. That's what proved she was a witch, Cook said. My father says there's no such thing as a witch. He says that nobody in Leiden is ever drowned or burnt for it now, not like the old days, when Cook was young. That was a long time ago."

"If your cook is so old, she must be needing help, then. I'm good and I'm fast." Lizzy couldn't let this awful boy ruin her chances. Maybe she could scare him into being quiet. "I think I should tell your mother how you tricked me onto the windmill." She brushed herself off. "I could have broken all my bones like that watchman did at the fire."

"You wouldn't tell her," he said, looking up from the paper he was marking. "Would you?"

She shrugged. "How old are you?" she asked.

"I am eight years old," he told her, "but I expect you're scared of me, anyway, because of what I did. I think you scare easy. I'm eight years and almost two months. I was born on the fifteenth of July, 1606. I go to school, but it's stupid. How old are you?"

"Twelve. But I'll be thirteen before the canals freeze." She was small for twelve, and people often thought she lied when she said it, but she didn't. Lying was a sin.

The wind shifted, and the windmill's sails began to slow. A man came walking out of the mist toward them.

The boy put down the chalk, picked up her shoe, and turned it over. "There's a hole in your sole," he told her. "My brother Adriaen is a shoemaker. Maybe he could fix it. Or," and he waved the shoe over the river, "I could just drop it in the water."

Lizzy moved fast. She grabbed her worn shoe from the boy's hand before he could let go. It was her only pair.

The wind shifted again, and the sails of the windmill slowed almost to a stop. Lizzy and the boy watched the man who'd come out of the mist begin to crank a wheel in front of the mill's steps. The mill revolved on a center post. By cranking the big wheel, the miller could turn the whole building around until the sails caught a better breeze. That was his job, to keep the sails going, not spinning so fast that the malt would burn, nor so slow that it wouldn't grind.

The man waved, and the boy waved back.

"You don't scare me," she told the boy. "I was brave

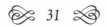

even when I was just a tot. My papa said so. It was in England we lived, in a village called Scrooby. Did you never hear of Scrooby?"

The boy shook his head. "I think you were scared on the windmill. It belongs to Sir my father. He is a miller. What does your father do?"

"My papa's recent dead," she told him. "My true mama was took with the fever when I wasn't much more than three."

"That makes you an orphan," the boy said. "I wish I was an orphan."

Lizzy brushed off her apron again with strong, swift strokes and shook her head. This boy really was a spoiled brat. Dutch children were far too free, and that was the truth of it. Master Brewster was right. "You said an evil thing," she told him. "And you're old enough to know better. You must honor your father and your mother."

The boy rolled up the paper he'd been marking and hopped down from the wall. "Well, if I was an orphan, nobody would make me go to school. My father makes me go to the Latin school. I hate it. I'd rather sit in the sty with the pigs all day than go to school."

Lizzy straightened her shoulders and started toward the house. "I'm going right now to ask your mother for work."

"You won't find her. She's almost as old as Cook is. She's forty-six years old and her bones creak, so she's not up and about yet. And Cook won't take you on without Madam my mother's say-so. You want to walk on my stilts?"

Lizzy wanted to, but she shook her head. This wasn't going well at all.

"How old were you in this Scrooby place," the boy asked, "when you brag you were so brave?"

"I was five years old. It was in the year of our Lord 1607, the year after you say you were born."

The boy shrugged and turned away. "What could you do, five years old?" he asked.

"I jumped in the Scrooby Manor moat is what," she told him, then caught her breath just remembering it.

"Oh!" He looked up. "Was the moat around a castle?" he asked. "Did you live in a castle? Were you a rich girl then, with pearls around your neck? Tell me."

This boy wanted to hear her talk, and Lizzy loved to tell stories about Scrooby, the ones her father had told her. So why not? If the tales pleased him, perhaps he wouldn't say mean things about her to his mother. Perhaps.

"Well, it wasn't a castle with turrets and dungeons and all," Lizzy began, "but I think that our manor house was very like a castle. Maybe not so big. Sit down," she said, "and I'll tell you." They sat down and leaned against the cool river wall.

She'd last seen the manor house when she was five

years old, but her father had described it at bedtime, over and over. "It was the archbishop who owned Scrooby Manor," she went on, "but Master William Brewster ran it. It had forty rooms, a great hall, and a chapel of its very own. There were kennels for the hunting dogs, a brewhouse, a bakehouse, two pools for fish, and a dovecote where fat pigeons roosted before they were baked into pigeon pie.

"It was a fine place, and don't think I'm just saying it. I know it was only in Scrooby, not in London, where the king lives. I know that. But kings of England had slept there. They had. And kings had hunted in its forest for at least four hundred years. It was the same forest that Robin Hood lived in with his Merry Men. That one."

"I've heard of Robin Hood," the boy said, leaning toward her. "The trader that sold us our new Turkish carpet, he told me all about Robin Hood, how he stole from the rich and gave to the poor. And how he got bled to death by a nun. I like stories. Go on. The moat."

"The moat," Lizzy said, and took a deep breath to call up the memories. "Well, it was on this cold October day. And the drawbridge of the moat—made of strong wood planks—it was let down so horsemen riding in from London could cross over. I was standing on it with the Farley boys. We were staring down at the water that wrapped around Scrooby Manor.

"The water had green skin. Eels swam in it. And whiskered fish. Maybe scaly dragons. John Farley always said they swam there, and he was seven, so we believed him. And that day, he saw one. 'Look,' he yelled to us, pointing, 'a baby dragon is heading under the bridge! See! Its tail is silver, with spikes at the end.'

"John's brother, Will, who was just my age, knelt at the edge of the bridge to look over. He pulled at my sleeve. 'I don't see it, Lizzy-bit. Do you?' He leaned out, trying to find the dragon's silver tail. My true name being Elizabeth, he called me Lizzy-bit. Even now, Will does," she explained to the boy. "And I *was* a wee bit of a thing, even when I was born. Because I was so little, Papa said he was always afraid I'd sicken and die."

"The moat," the boy urged. "And the dragon."

"Yes." She grinned at him. "Well, the bridge over the moat was high. The water was far down. None of us could swim. But Will wanted so much to see the dragon that he leaned out even farther. He teetered over the boards of the bridge. . . ."

"And he *fell*," the boy said. "He fell right in that scummy moat."

"He did just that," Lizzy told him. "And as he fell, he cried out, 'Lizzy-bit!' He landed with a huge splash. When his head poked up out of the green water, he didn't scream and he didn't call out; but he looked so scared that, without even thinking, I closed my eyes, spread out my arms, and I belly flopped in after him."

The boy laughed. "You were a fool even then," he told her, but he leaned forward and waited for more.

Lizzy took a breath. "I still remember the sting I felt when I hit. And I sank. Under the water, I could feel something wrap around my leg. Maybe an eel. Maybe the tongue of a scaly dragon."

She rubbed her scraped chin. It was damp with blood. The mist was burning off the field. A little girl of the house, out rolling a hoop in the yard, called to the boy that it was time for school.

"What happened next?" The boy leaned toward her, waiting.

"It's a long story," she said. "That's just the beginning. It goes all the way from Scrooby there to Stink Alley, near St. Peter's Church, here. That's where I live now with the William Brewster family. I hear your sister calling. Is it your sister?"

"Lysbet, yes, but what happened?"

"I'll tell you tomorrow." Lizzy smiled. "If your mother hires me. If I don't tell her you tried to kill me."

He smiled. "Is it a scary story? I especially like scary stories."

"It's both long and scary." Lizzy started toward the

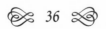

house. "It's got spies. People get thrown in jail. There's a storm at sea."

The boy thought about it. "I have to go to school. But I'll meet you here tomorrow morning. I'll go tell Madam my mother to take you on, and she will. She listens to me. She bought the Turkish rug only because I liked it. Who was it you said sent you? Clara?"

"Over at the Van Heusdens'," Lizzy told him.

He ran toward the house, well ahead. "Madam my mother has seven children still alive," he called back. "But I'm her very favorite."

Chapter Six

"YOU DID IT, Lizzy-bit!" Will Farley's changing voice cracked from soprano to bass. "I knew you'd find work."

Lizzy curtsied to him, laughing. "I did, kind sir."

Will looked taller tonight. His knees were almost poking through his stockings, and for certain he couldn't wear that doublet much longer. His face was drawn, but not tight with anger and sickness, the way it had been yesterday.

"I'm sorry for shouting at you," he told her. "My head was beating like a tambourine."

"You frightened me." She lowered her voice. "Those things you said. Have you lost your faith, then?"

"Nay, I still believe the Gospel with all my heart," he

told her. "But we came here to live by it, not to slowly die for it. And that's what I think."

The light was growing dim on the square around St. Peter's Church, and the shops that bordered it were closing. In the few minutes left before supper, Lizzy and Will were tending Love Brewster. After they ate, Will would stay for lessons. Will's parents could neither read nor write, and the Separatists felt that both were important for boys to learn. That is why he and his brother came to study with Master Brewster when time let them. And those few nights when Will was at Stink Alley, it felt to Lizzy like home.

"Look at *me!*" Love called to them. "Let's do Hunt the Fox! I'm Fox. Lizzy, you and Will chase me. Home is the bell tower. I'll beat you there!" Without waiting, he ran.

"But look at *you!*" Will said to Lizzy, smiling. "How'd a cook ever come to hire a mite like you? I venture you made her that tasty rosewater cheesecake that Sally taught you. Or the marzipan. Anyway, I'm proud of you."

And Will was proud of her. What's more, he told her so, like Papa and Sally would have. Her papa had married Sally, the Scrooby Manor cook, soon after Lizzy had jumped in the moat. Almost at once, Sally'd had her chopping onions, stirring custards, rolling piecrusts, and turning chickens, mutton joints, and rabbits on the fireplace spit. To keep her out of trouble, Sally had said. But it was more than that. Sally had loved her. But she was dead now. Shivering and sweating and coughing up blood, she died just four months before Papa was taken. Only Will knew how very much she missed them.

Lizzy told Will about the cheeky little miller's son, how he'd tricked her onto the windmill. She'd told him about how, before she'd even set eyes on the boy's mother, Madam Cornelia, she had sent word that Cook was to take her on, how truly it was the boy who got her hired, not any fancy dish. She would have kept talking, trying to cheer Will, but Love came running back.

"I'm the *Fox*!" he shouted again, but still no one chased him. He stuck out his bottom lip.

"Remember how we used to play Hunt the Fox in Scrooby?" Lizzy asked Will as they walked around the square. "On those hot summer nights in the courtyard. You always won. But it was no fair. Your legs were longer." She rested her hand on his arm, laughing.

He pulled away from her touch, his face suddenly red. "I didn't stink so much then, either," he said, shaking his head.

"Everybody stinks some," Lizzy told him, folding her arms. She hadn't meant to startle him. "Besides, you won't always. You'll get a job doing . . . I don't know . . . something else."

He nodded. "I will at that," he said. "John and me,

we've been talking. Our heads aren't clear yet on what to do, but . . ."

Love was jumping up and down on the cobblestones. "Catch me, then, if you *can!*" he called. He said it in Dutch, which he'd learned from playing with neighbor boys, but Will and Lizzy understood him. While they always spoke English in their houses, their Dutch was just as solid. Pastor Robinson and the elders knew that if they were to settle well in Holland, if they were to draw people to their beliefs, they would have to speak Dutch. They encouraged their children to learn it. *"Vang me, dan, als je kan!"* Love called again.

Suddenly, Will reached his arms out wide. "Catch *you?* Better watch out! Here I come!" He ran three strides after the Fox, but then fell back to walk again with Lizzy. "My legs won't do it, Lizzy-bit," he told her. "Too much stomping on wet wool. If the Devil himself thumbed his nose at me, I couldn't turn tail and run. These legs aren't mine. They belong to some old man who creaks when he sits."

"I won! I won!" Love called from a distance. "Where *are* you?"

"Wait here," Lizzy told Will. She hurried to the church bell tower after Love, scooped him up from his hiding place, and carried him back as he wiggled under her arm.

Will was waiting for them at the church door.

"Let's do it again," Love said. "This time, *you* be Fox."

Will cocked his head at Love, smiled mysteriously, and held out two tightly closed fists. "Forget the Fox, Master Love. I'll play you a game of Ho Go. Which hand do you choose?"

Love forgot the Fox. Ho Go was a really good game. If you chose right, you got something. He studied the two fists closely, turning them over so he could see top and bottom. Finally, he ran his fingers over the knuckles of Will's right hand. "Go," he said.

Will turned his fist over and opened it slowly. Inside was a shiny brown clay marble. Then he opened the other hand. It was empty. "You chose well," Will told him. "This is my favorite marble." He rolled it around in his palm. "I brought five of them from England. This is the last, and now it's yours."

"Ohhhhhh. It's a *knicker!*" "Knicker" was the Dutch word for "marble," and Love had gotten in the habit of using it. He sucked in his breath. The most he'd hoped for was a sweet raisin. He plucked his treasure off Will's palm.

"Will, are you sure?" Lizzy asked. "Love's a baby. He loses things. You were always so good at Ring Taw, and Lag and Holy Bang, too. You should keep it."

"I am *not* a baby. Wrestling is the baby," Love said. He lay on his stomach and rolled his new marble between the cobblestones like a boat floating down a crisscross of canals.

Will shrugged. "I'm too big for marbles. Can't kneel down to shoot them now anyway, can I?"

"That was kind of you," Lizzy told him. "I'll teach Love how to play Ring Taw with it."

Will leaned back against the church door. "So, Lizzy-bit, tell me about your new job. How do you get on with the cook? Does she like to shoot knickers?"

"Oh, Will," Lizzy said, "I know she drinks vinegar instead of beer. I never saw a cook so sour. I did everything she set me to, and I did it fast and I did it with a shut-up mouth. She didn't tell me *not* to come back, so I will. Tomorrow, I'll be even faster and better."

Chapter Seven

*A*T THE BREWSTERS' house, the whale-oil lamps were already lit, adding their smoky light to the glow of the fireplace. Under the open window, the gate-leg table was spread with a white cloth. Supper was cheese flavored with cumin and chunks of dense dark bread and boiled pike stew with parsnips, prunes, and cabbage in it.

Baby Wrestling lay fretting in his cradle. Master and Mistress Brewster sat on the long bench facing the table. There was room enough for Patience and Fear on the bench, but the rest of the children—Love, Lizzy, and Will—stood to eat, as they always did. Lizzy could see Will's old-man's knees shaking. Fear ladled a portion of stew onto each of their wooden plates.

Master Brewster bowed his gray head. He asked blessings on the food, warned them sternly of sins that lay in wait, and gave thanks for the love of God and the goodness of their lives. Patience leaned low and bowed her head deep toward the pungent stew, away from the smell of Will.

"Amen," they all said, and opened their eyes. The white walls of the room glowed with reflected light.

They all were hungry and ate fast, spearing the parsnips with their knives. Using wooden spoons, they lifted the flaking chunks of warm, oily pike to their mouths, carefully picking out all the tiny bones they could find. The slippery prunes they ate with their fingers.

"Fetch the tankard, please, Patience," Mary Brewster asked. Patience filled a tall pewter tankard from the beer keg and brought it to her mother. After the adults had drunk their fill, the mug was passed on to the children. Most water came from the canals and rivers. No one drank it. Slops and chamber pots were emptied there, even though it was against the law. They cooked with rainwater that collected under the house in a cistern, but beer was the family's drink, morning, noon, and night.

Master Brewster wiped his hands and dabbed his trim mustache and goatee on his napkin. He lifted his head and once again offered a prayer of thanks.

"Amen," they said together again. "Amen."

Then Master Brewster turned to Will. "Your father looked poorly at Meeting last night," he said. "Is he unwell?"

Will looked pasty, too. Couldn't Master Brewster see it? Lizzy wondered. She listened closely to their talk as she and the girls cleared the table and wiped the plates clean.

"Well as can be, Master Brewster," Will said. He hesitated. "My pa is deep in the faith, but . . ."

"But?"

"I think—no, I know for certain—Pa misses following the plow. City life is poison to him. It tries him sorely."

"We were meant to come, Will," Master Brewster told him. "The hand of God led us here."

Lizzy hoped Will wasn't going to argue. He'd never win. Master Brewster was not a big man. He'd never labored with his arms and legs. He hadn't needed to. His father had left him money enough for his family to live on. It was his mind that was strong. Not many tried to match wits with him.

"But my pa," Will went on, staring at the floor, "all these years, my pa never learnt Dutch, so except at Meetings to praise God and at home to say how he misses the farm, he hardly talks from one day's start to the next. And he can't go back, can he?" He looked up, pained. "They'd clap him in jail."

"Go back to Scrooby? Of course he can't go back."

William Brewster put his hand on Will's shoulder. "I'll counsel him," he said. "And I want you to speak strongly to your brother, John."

"John, sir?" Will was wary.

"He is not here for lessons tonight." He leveled his eyes at Will. "Why?"

Will paused.

I can read his eyes, Lizzy thought. He's trying to decide if he should lie. He had better not.

"Well, sir," Will began, "John was tired. *Is* tired. He works hard all day."

"We are all tired at the end of a long day. But we are never too weary to praise God. Does he not thirst to read the Word for himself?"

"Yes, sir. But, sir," Will went on, "I fear John finds reading and writing a very great trial."

"I'm aware of that. But he must learn to read the Scriptures," Master Brewster told him. "You are doing well. Very well. If you are steadfast and do not fall to the free habits of Dutch youth, you might well become a scholar and perhaps even an elder."

"Thank you, sir." Will glanced at Lizzy, took a deep breath, and bowed briefly. "I'll get the Bible." Every family in the congregation had a Bible, even if no one could read it. William Brewster, though, had shelves of books, more than a hundred. Some of them were in Latin. Lizzy wondered if the miller's boy could read them.

While Will fetched the Bible, William Brewster turned to her. "Elizabeth, I understand that you found employment today. A milling family, I hear. Is it a good and wholesome place? What do you know of their faith? How do they observe the Sabbath?" he asked.

"I . . . I don't know, sir," she stammered. "The boy of the house told me they go to St. Peter's Church on Sunday morning, but for the rest . . ."

"It is your duty to instruct them that the *entire* Sabbath day is holy. Too many Dutch are lax in this. My days are much occupied, but I will speak to your employer soon. You may continue in this for now. Make no plans, however, to remain until I am completely satisfied with the sanctity of their house."

She nodded. Surely he would approve. Madame Cornelia seemed a good person, and perhaps he would never meet the sassy boy.

He gave her a long, steady look. "Elizabeth, you are almost grown. Satan will soon begin to tempt you mightily. It may be that your father's pampering has weakened you to Dutch temptations. Be watchful. Every day you must live a life worthy of a saint."

"Yes, Master Brewster," she said. "I will do. Every day all day, I pray to be good." And she did. If only she could be sure what good was.

As she started up the stairs to bed with Fear and Love, Lizzy could hear Will reading aloud, one word carefully placed after the other, "'And the Lord said unto Satan, Whence commest thou? And Satan answered the Lord, saying, From compassing the earth to and fro, and from walking in it.'"

From the step above, Love leaned back and whispered in Lizzy's ear, "I heard what Father said. He said Satan's after *you*. Satan's going to wake you and hold your nose. Satan's going to shake you and eat your toes."

Lizzy shivered. Upstairs in the dark, Fear hugged her tightly. "He's just teasing," Lizzy told her. "It's all right." Yet her eyes searched the corners of the room. She could still hear Will reading from the Book of Job. She had heard it often at Meeting. Satan was compassing the earth to and fro. He was walking in it. She was almost sure that at this very moment, crouched deep in the shadows, Satan was watching.

Chapter Eight

*L*IZZY WOKE EARLY. What with the skittering mice and Fear shaking her awake to hear them, it had been another restless night. And then there was Will. She kept thinking of Will and his creaking knees, not able to shoot marbles anymore.

When she reached the Gerritzen place, the boy was sitting on the river wall. She smiled and waved. He'd gotten her the job.

The boy looked closely at her in the early dim light.

"Yesterday, your apron was just dirty," he told her. "Today, it's dirtier. Your cap's almost off again and your hair looks like a starling's nest."

"Good morrow to you, too," Lizzy said. "My apron got all soaked with blood yesterday. I tried to wash it out in the canal, but blood leaves a stain. Yesterday, I wrung three chickens' necks; that's why it happened. Cook didn't like it that you got me hired, you know. She said you're spoiled. Then she told me her chopping cleaver was lost, and she set me to wringing the hens' necks, plucking their feathers, cleaning them out, and cutting them up. I think she wanted me to say I couldn't kill them without a cleaver."

She looked him over. Next to him on the wall sat his paper and chalk. "Are you off to school so soon?" she asked.

"I go to school as late as I can, " he said. "I was hoping you'd come early. I was waiting for the story. I was calling it 'Lizzy's story.'"

"You remembered my name." She smiled. "What's yours?" she asked him.

"Won't tell you, will I? It's stupid and old-fashioned. The dumb boys at school tease me about it. My brothers all have proper names like Willem and Cornelis, but Sir my father and Madam my mother went dotty when they chose mine."

The boy began to mark on his paper. "I rode the windmill all the way round this morning," he told her.

"You did not."

"Did too. I'll show you how sometime. And then I'll dare you do it. Then I'll dare you swim to America. Have you heard about America? There's a north part and a south part. Sir my father has a map that shows it. You wouldn't know this, but in the middle of the ocean between here and there is a monster golden fish with a waterspout. The natives in America are all cannibals. They cut off bits of you and make you watch as they fry the pieces and eat you up. I'll never go there. How do you wring a chicken's neck? Don't they peck your wrist?"

Lizzy grinned. She liked the boy. He talked too much, the way she did. "I guess a spoiled miller's boy like you doesn't need to kill chickens. It's not so hard. What you do is grab the head tight so it doesn't peck. Then you swing it round and round, sprightly like. My hands are strong like Papa's are." She caught her breath. "Like Papa's were, rest his soul," she said softly. Then she raised her chin. She had promised Papa she would be strong.

The boy leaned forward, listening. "What you do," she went on, "is you keep a fast hold on the chicken's neck and then give a quick jerk. The neck makes a fearful crack when it breaks, and you've got a limp head in your hand. When you let go, the poor clucker runs around wild in the yard like—"

"A chicken with its head wrung off!"

"So they say." Lizzy smiled. "Now I best go in."

"Wait!" the boy told her. "That wasn't Lizzy's story. That was just about chickens. I want the good one. The work bell hasn't rung yet. Cook's still snoring. And you promised. What happened when you jumped in the moat? Did you really think you could save that boy?"

"It was Will. I had to try," Lizzy said. She sat down on the hard ground and glanced up at him on the wall. She found she was looking forward to telling the story. It would help her bring Papa closer. "Well, then," she began, "I jumped in. Flat. The water in the moat was cold. It wasn't deep, but it was higher than I am, even now. And thick, thicker than cabbage stew. When I sank under, something slippery curled round my leg, but I kicked it free."

The boy jumped off the wall and sat next to her. "I think it was an eel," he said. "That's what I think."

"Or a shy dragon," she went on, grinning at him. "I wasn't under long enough to see. When I popped up, I sucked in some air and looked for Will, hoping he wasn't still under the slime. He wasn't. He was paddling, splashing, like big dogs do, over toward the steep bank. I choked and coughed, and got water in my nose, but I wasn't going to drown. I paddled and kicked, just the way Will had, until I got to him.

"From the edge of the steep shore, he pulled my slippery arm with one hand. With the other one, he held his nose." Lizzy laughed.

"Did you stink?" the boy asked.

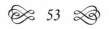 53

"We both did. The moat's where they emptied chamber pots. Like you do in canals. And fish tails and slops the pigs wouldn't touch. Rats swam in the water, too. I think they liked the smell.

"John stood on the bridge and laughed at us. Then he ran off home without telling, leaving us shivering beside the moat. Later, he got a good switching. Being seven years old, he should have known better."

"*You* should have known better," the boy told her.

"That's what Papa said. He even brushed my backside with a birch stick, but it didn't hurt. Then he took me to the River Ryton, which ran behind Scrooby Manor, where the water ran clear. He dunked me up and down to get the green scum off and scrubbed me pink with a brush and soap a chambermaid had given him. But the stench hung on."

The boy sniffed. "You still stink."

"I do not. That was seven years ago. But I think it was the stink that made me sick. Papa said he was sure I was dying. For three weeks, Papa said, I lay in the straw in the stable. You see, I wasn't a grand girl in a castle. My papa shod the Scrooby Manor horses. My mama dead and gone and all, he kept me close by in the stable when I was sick.

"I think that's when Papa decided to marry Sally. She was the cook at the manor house, and she boiled up a pot of onion juice and bathed my head and mouth and nose with it. One good stink to fight another. Still, I threw up a lot.

"Will Farley didn't sicken. He and John came by the stable to see me. John called me 'Missy Puke Stockings.'"

"I don't like the part about your being sick," the boy said. He got up, sat across from her, unrolled his paper again, and sharpened his chalk on a stone. "You said there were spies," he went on. "Tell about the spies."

"What are you writing on that paper?" she asked him. "Are you doing sums?"

"Waste my paper on sums? Sums are almost as stupid as Latin. This is harder than sums." He rested the paper on a piece of wood. "Do sit still. And go on. I can still have you sent home, you know. I can tell how you rode the windmill."

"And I can tell how you made me do it," Lizzy said. She wanted to stick out her tongue, but instead she sighed. The Yarn Market's work bell hadn't rung yet. There was still time. "All right, the spies," she said.

"In England, we had enemies. Especially Master Brewster. We were all afraid for him. If the spies found out what he was up to, the king could order his ears sliced off. Or his nose split up the middle. The king sometimes did that. If you disobeyed, the king's men might sear your forehead with a hot brand. Then everybody you met could see by your scars that you were stirring people up against the king. They'd already fined Master Brewster once, a whole year's wages. His wife, Mary, had a new baby girl then. They named her Fear."

The boy looked up from his paper. "Is this a true story?"

"It is. I sleep in the same bed as Fear does here, in Stink Alley. And her sister Patience." She gave her apron a flap. "Are you writing in Latin with that chalk?"

He waved her question away. "That man. His name is Brewster? What did he do? Did he kill a man? How did he? Poison? A dagger? Did he snap somebody's neck in the dark?"

"Master Brewster does not kill. He obeys all the commandments. He's a very, very pious man. What he did was he wouldn't go to the king's church. The king said you had to go to his church or else."

The boy yawned and rolled his eyes, as if she'd said Master Brewster had been caught twiddling his thumbs.

Lizzy leaned forward. "Don't look like that! It was no little thing! There was a big group of us who wouldn't go to the king's church in Scrooby. It had a preacher the bishop had put there, not one of our own. They sang in harmony there, and danced down the aisle with bells on their toes on holy days. They wore collars stiff with starch, and that's the Devil's liquor. For music, they played an organ, and that's the Devil's bagpipes. We didn't want anything to do with them. So we had our own

Meetings in Scrooby Manor. We prayed pure and simple as God intended, not the king.

"People in the town turned on us. They watched us day and night. They were out to get the whole lot, some fifty of us, Papa and me included. When we walked to the manor house on the Lord's Day, nice as you please, they threw stones at us. Knocked John Farley out cold once. They called us names.

"Even the king called us names. He said we were 'sour, bloodless, stonyhearted bigots.' Imagine him calling us that, when that's what *he* was. That's what Master Brewster said. But Master Brewster said it low, and he was careful who he said it to. The walls had ears."

"Brewster, the man's name is?" the boy asked.

"I've said it many times. William Brewster."

"Can he read and write?" the boy asked.

"Of course he can read and write. In English and Latin both. Greek, too, I think. And by now, Dutch. He and William Bradford, too, who came over with us."

The boy scrolled up his paper and tucked it in the leather pouch that hung on his belt. "What happened about the spies?"

"Well, the moat and the river kept out robbers and highwaymen, but not spies. Since the manor house was a post station, the spies could walk right over the draw-bridge, pay for a bed, and stay the night. You couldn't tell spies from friends. Except Papa said they smiled more.

"I saw one myself," Lizzy told him. "I did. One night when I got better, I lay by the fireplace in the great hall. I curled up small and I listened while the men of the congregation drank beer by the fire and worried over how to get out of England. To go, you had to have a permit. To get a permit, you had to say why you were going. If you said why truly, you'd get clapped in jail.

"'Holland's the place,' one of them whispered. 'We can pray as we want and they can't reach us there.'

"'But how do you say "I want a job" in Dutch?' my papa asked. 'And how do we get from here to there?'

"A stranger just in from his ride on the Great North Road from London took his ale across the great hall to join them. 'Cheers!' said he, and he raised his leather mug. 'Going from here to where?' he asked with a smile. It was an easy smile, Papa said, too broad and easy, the smile of a fox, the smile of a spy."

"I know that kind of smile," the boy told Lizzy. "I saw it yesterday on two men in the printing shop where I go for my paper. It's this place called In the Printery. These men, their Dutch wasn't good. They were asking too many questions, so the printers were wary and didn't answer back. They said they were looking for some man named William Brewster."

Chapter Nine

"YOU ARE MAKING that up," Lizzy said, but her heart jumped. "That's a lie, and lying is a sin."

"I tell lies sometimes—when I have to," the boy told her. "But this is true. Heart's truth!" He put his hand on his heart to swear to it. "The men had long, thin daggers," he went on. "And fancy swords. And the man they called Brewster, they said he is here . . . illegally."

"That is not true!" Lizzy leaned toward him. "The Dutch let in honest people. And we've got papers that say we can stay safe and sound unless we break laws, and we don't." She shook her head. "Master Brewster is—"

"Those men," he interrupted her, "said this Brewster's a criminal in England. They said he wrote lies about the king of England in these little books, that he sent them to England. They said he's dangerous. They said it in that funny way English people do when they try to talk Dutch. And then they smiled that smile. And they said, oh, they meant him no harm, but you could tell they did."

Lizzy stood up. She felt as though she should run, but her legs were limp. We're *safe* here, she thought. Nobody's ever been afraid here. The king's arm can't reach this far. He's not king here. Or can kings reach anywhere they want to? she thought with a start. What if they took Master Brewster back to England? What would happen to Fear and Love and baby Wrestling? What would happen to us all?

"I don't know what he writes," she told the boy. "He doesn't like the king, of course. But he only writes the truth. He doesn't lie."

"These men told the printers that just last month he sent this big pack of lies to England in wine barrels," the boy went on. "And they said, 'Here's one,' and they flipped this little pamphlet in the printers' faces. I was standing right there. And I said that was stupid, that the words would get all washed off by the wine, and they laughed at me. And they said, 'Ha ha ha, what a dumb little brat,' because this pack of lies was hid in *fake* bottoms, not where the wine sloshed about at all." The boy took a breath. "I'm not a dumb brat."

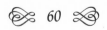 60

"You talked to them? You didn't tell them anything, did you?"

He smiled and waited. "You mean like say I know who lives in Stink Alley, near St. Peter's Church?"

"You didn't!"

"They called me a dumb brat. I wouldn't tell them anything."

"This was yesterday? They've come all the way to Leiden? Maybe it's too late," Lizzy said, her voice rising. "I didn't know anybody was looking for him. But then, he wouldn't have told *me*, would he? What if they want him dead? I've got to warn him right now." She turned at once to go.

"You'll be late to work if you do. You'll lose your job," the boy told her. "Nothing I can do. Cook'll say you're a sluggard."

"I want to work in your mother's kitchen. I need to. But what if they kidnap Master Brewster and take him back to England and try him in the king's court? They'll say he's guilty of something and cut off his ears. Or what if they hang him by his neck just because he wrote down the plain truth? It would be my fault, then, wouldn't it, because I hadn't warned him?"

The boy didn't say no.

"He may be at home writing," she told him. "He does that some mornings. No matter, I've got to go there," she

said, and started off at a trot toward Stink Alley. He kept pace with her.

"Stop a minute." He grabbed her arm, but she jerked it away. "No, wait," he said. "At least slow down."

Lizzy frowned, but she stopped. She had to. The narrow street by the canal was blocked by a wagon unloading barrel after barrel into the tavern there. Nothing to do but wait. She crossed and uncrossed her arms. "Well?" she asked the boy.

"What if I told Cook that Madam my mother sent you away to get something?"

"Sent me for what?" she asked.

The boy thought. "It couldn't be for just anything," he said. "Something Cook needs." They were near the university, and students waited with them for the wagon to pass, chatting, in no hurry. People on their way to work to make felt hats, weave corduroy, or cobble shoes greeted each other with "*Goede morgen.*" The work bell in the Yarn Market would soon be ringing. Time was flying fast and she was standing still. Lizzy wished she could fly over the wagon or crawl under it. The men were laughing, taking their time.

"Think of something," he told her. "Think. What does Cook need—besides a smile?"

"All I know is, a man's coming for supper tonight, somebody special," Lizzy told him. "A brewer. He buys a lot of your father's malt. I'm to roast a big hare on the spit for it. I heard Cook and your mother talking. Your mother said this man likes those spicy cookies filled with almond paste. Cook said, well, she didn't know how to make those. She said rice pudding would do just fine."

"I hate rice pudding. She makes it every day. It tastes like pap. Well, do we need rice, then?" the boy asked.

The last barrel was rolling into the tavern. "No. But those cookies. I know where to get them."

"All right," the boy said. "That's a plan. What I'll do right now is go back to Cook and tell her you went to get those cookies before starting the hare. I'll tell her Madam my mother told me to tell you to get them." He grinned. "Of course that's a lie."

Her heart fell.

"What if you save his life?" he went on. "Won't a little lie be worth it? Besides, it's my lie, not yours. Pick up twenty cookies on the way back. I like them."

The wagon creaked, then the wheels turned, and a lazy horse began to pull it away. Lizzy didn't move. "I wouldn't be lying to save his life, but to save my job."

He shrugged. "I'm sure that Madam my mother *really* would want those cookies. And that's the truth."

"I just don't know. It might do," she told him. "It might. Do you have any money?"

"No. I bought some red chalk yesterday." He bit his lip.

"Can't you just pay them later?"

"Maybe. I think they'll trust me." Lizzy started down the street, then turned back. "You don't have to lie for me. Don't do it." But the boy had gone.

As she threaded her way through the crowd, the bell in the Yarn Market began to toll.

Dodging late workers and shop women sweeping the street, Lizzy retraced her morning path. It took her just under ten minutes, running flat out, to reach Stink Alley. She got there winded, hardly able to speak. But as soon as she flung open the door, she gasped, "Master Brewster's in danger. He must go into hiding. There are spies!"

But he wasn't there. He was away, teaching English to a university student. Mistress Brewster stopped twisting the wool on her spindle, calmed Lizzy down, then listened closely as she told the story. Lizzy looked for fear in her eyes, but if Mary Brewster was afraid, she hid it. She lifted the crying baby, Wrestling, away from Patience and told her daughter to go at once, find her father, and tell him exactly what the boy had heard.

"It's doubtless nothing, Elizabeth," Mistress Brewster told her when Patience had gone. "It may be the boy's imagination. We had not heard of unwanted visitors from abroad. Now, go back to your work. Explain to the cook. She'll understand."

Understand, maybe, Lizzy thought. But forgive, never,

unless the boy's plan worked. Her shirt was damp through with sweat. What if it really was just the boy's imagination? Or, worse, his joke?

Again she ran. This time, she headed for the Blaeus' bakery, where she'd gotten the fancy bread and letter cookies. They'd trust her, surely.

Jan was sweeping the walk in front of the shop.

"Lizzy!" He smiled and leaned on the broom. His face was smudged with soot. But when he saw the anxious look on Lizzy's face, his own fell.

"What's wrong?" he asked. "Is all not well?"

Lizzy took a deep breath. "Jan, I need some help. Yesterday, I got a kitchen job, but now I'm late, for good reason, truly. Cook is so ill-tempered, though, I'm afraid she'll fret and fume, and then let me go." She looked about frantically. "Is your mother here? I must take back cookies, the spicy ones filled with almond paste, to explain why I was late. Is she here?"

Jan laughed and brushed the tops of her shoes with his broom. "Is that all, Lizzy? Slow down," he said, grinning. "If that dragon cook starts to breathe flames at you, just ring the alarm. I'll pull out my trusty leather bucket and douse her with canal water."

Lizzy tried to smile.

"You want the *speculaas* filled with almond paste?" he asked.

She nodded, her lips tight.

"There are some left, I think. My mother's ailing this morning, but she made a batch of them yesterday. You have a cloth to carry them in?"

She shook her head. "Can we heap them in my apron?" They both looked her apron over. It was stained with blood and dirt.

He laughed, hurried into the shop, and came out shortly with a worn white cloth folded into a package. "There are eleven cookies in here," he said. "All that's left. Since they're yesterday's, that'll just be nine duiten."

"Oh." She'd forgotten. "I don't have any money, Jan, I'm sorry. I'll pay you when I bring the cloth back. May I? Please."

"On credit? I'm not sure," he said, and turned away into the shop.

Lizzy's heart sank. Did Jan not trust her? What could she have done?

But when he came back, she saw the glint in his eye. He'd been teasing, and it was no time for fun. He handed her a small sugar pancake. "Only if you eat this as you go," he said, grinning.

She took the pancake and the package, smiled her thanks, and ran.

Chapter Ten

*T*HE BOY WAS NOT THERE by the river wall. He was at
school by now, hating sums, Lizzy thought. What
had he told Cook? Had he lied for her? If he had, it was
her fault and her sin really. But she only half hoped he
hadn't.

She darted through the windmill yard to the house,
weaving past horses and barking dogs and men hauling
sacks in wheelbarrows, cradling her package carefully.

Cook stood waiting at the door with her arms crossed,
a switch in her hand. She was heavy and bent. Wisps of
white hair fringed out from under her oil-stained cap. All
Lizzy could see in her face was anger.

"You're late," Cook snapped, and flicked the switch
sharply at Lizzy's ankles. "What kind of lazy house do you

think this is? Did that rascal boy tell you you'd have it easy here?" She raised the switch.

Lizzy did not flinch. She would not give Cook that satisfaction. Cook had not told her to leave, so she made a small curtsy, unfolded the cloth, and held it out to her. "These are the almond cookies the young Master sent me to get. The man who is coming to dinner especially likes them." The boy did tell her to go. This was not quite a lie. Lies were slippery things. She took a deep breath. "He said he'd tell you. Did he not? I hurried." She looked up to see how Cook was taking this.

Cook poked at the cookies and wrinkled her nose as if they smelt like spoiled fish. "Oh, that rascal told me he sent you off, but I think he's the one who wanted the cookies. They don't look fresh. How much did you pay?" she asked.

"Nine duiten. But I didn't have the money. So I—"

"*Nine* duiten! Well!" Cook sniffed. "You're not going to get that from me. No matter what that spoiled scamp said, *I* never asked you to hightail it off to fetch this garbage." She took the cookies, then ate one, making a sour face. But, Lizzy noted, she finished it and licked her fingers. "I ought to send you home right now," she went on. "That's what I ought. And I would, too, but there's too much work to do." She flicked the switch in front of Lizzy's feet. "Inside!"

Lizzy wiped the loose damp hair out of her eyes and hurried into the kitchen. Cook set out a cleaver and a rusty knife.

"Use these, and get to work," she said. Tight-lipped, she jerked her head toward a meat hook on the ceiling. The carcass of a lean brown hare hung there, its hind legs tied, its long ears sagging. A farmer had brought it in three days before, and tonight it would be supper.

Lizzy stared up at the hare and bit her lip. There was nothing more she could do for Master Brewster. She'd try to put the spies out of her mind and show Cook what a help she'd be. She moved a three-legged stool under the hare, stepped up and lifted it off the hook, then hopped down and laid it on the cutting board. Cook watched, arms crossed, as Lizzy raised the cleaver high and with one swift stroke lopped off both the hare's front paws.

The rusty knife Cook had set out wouldn't slice butter, but to say so would be to find fault, and Cook would surely bristle. Using it, though, would take twice the time, so turning away to keep Cook from seeing, Lizzy pushed the rusty knife under a pile of onions. Then she slipped her own small knife out of the woolen bag that hung at her waist. Neatly, with her newly sharpened knife, she slit through the skin around the hare's hind leg joints. Then, stepping on the stool, she hung the carcass back up and, starting at its ankles, peeled off its furry pelt as easily as she pulled off her own stockings. She rolled the skin all the way down to the head. Lifting the hare off the hook again, she hopped down, placed it carefully on the board, and chopped off its head in a single blow. Some cooks left the head on till serving time, but she cut it off, the way Sally always had.

Humming as she worked, she sliced open the chest, scooped out the entrails, and set them aside to feed the hogs—all save the heart and liver, which she could add later to meatballs.

There. That was fast, faster than I've ever done before, she thought, grinning. And neat, too. Sally would have said she was splendid. Master Brewster would say she was showing off.

She turned to see if Cook was pleased. But Cook had stopped watching.

As she rubbed the meat with vinegar, Lizzy waited to hear Cook tell her sharply that she was doing everything wrong.

Cook remained silent, though, staring out the kitchen door.

Well, then, I won't say anything, either, Lizzy thought. I'll keep my tongue tied tight.

A big black cat slinked in the kitchen door past Cook. It rubbed its head back and forth against Lizzy's ankle, so she pinched off a piece of liver and tossed it on the tile floor. The cat licked up the chunk, purred, and pawed her leg for more.

And now to the larding of the hare. Lizzy had done this scores of times, and it was, of course, Sally who'd shown her how to do it so slick and easy.

Hares were bigger and tougher than rabbits and needed extra fat. You pulled strips of lard through the lean, dry meat to make it moist and juicy. Lizzy cut twenty lardoons, long thin pieces of pork back fat, threaded them one by one into a larding needle, and pulled each strand through the tough hare meat. Then she rubbed the hare all over with salt and a heavy grating of nutmeg and trussed it up deftly with a needle and thread from her pouch.

If only she'd been here to watch, Lizzy thought, Cook would have seen how good I can do. But Cook was gone, in the backyard with the chickens.

Lizzy was set to skewer the hare, aiming the long iron spit at the hollow of its body, when she heard the scream—a high, sharp, fearsome shriek, as though somebody had stepped on a fireplace coal. It stopped, then began again, stronger.

Lizzy dropped the hare on the cutting board and ran out the kitchen door into the small backyard. There, curled on the ground, two dogs barking at her side, was Cook, clutching her ankle, writhing in pain.

When she saw Lizzy, she screamed louder.

The cook's shrieks were so loud, they reached the boy's mother, Madam Cornelia, who was sitting on a bench in front of the house, knitting slowly. She hurried into the back garden as quickly as her arthritic bones would let her.

"Gertrude," Madam Cornelia said, holding her hand to her throat, "what happened?" Wincing at the pain in her knees, she bent down, her arm around the cook's shoulder. "Are you hurt?" she asked gently.

"She's a witch! Not a girl. She's a witch!" Cook's eyes opened wide with fear as she pointed straight at Lizzy.

Chapter Eleven

SURELY COOK HAD LOST her senses. Lizzy couldn't believe what she'd heard. "Please, madam," Lizzy said, hurrying toward her, "please, I've not done anything wrong. I was just about to set the hare on the spit."

"In my kitchen! A *witch*!" Cook screamed. "I knew from the start she had the evil eye. Yesterday, the milk curdled and turned green, so I had to throw it to the pigs."

Madam Cornelia shook her head in distress.

Could she really believe I curdle milk? Lizzy wondered. "Madam," she said urgently, "I can't think what Cook means."

Cook, still heaving out cries, peeled down her stocking and held her bare foot out for Madam Cornelia to see, as though this was proof of her charge. The foot was purple and yellow at the arch, growing puffy and fat.

"I'll tell you," Cook whispered to Madam Cornelia, pulling her close. "I'll tell you exactly what I seen." Lizzy moved forward to listen. "I set that baggage to skinning a hare, and she pushed my knife aside. I saw it with my own holy eyes. Then she slit that hare down the middle with nothing but her sharp cat claws. Did it quicker than a pure girl could with a knife."

Lizzy stepped in closer. "But, madam, please, she didn't see—"

"Away! Away!" Cook moaned and crossed her arms in front of her face. "She shoots me with pain. Child of the Devil."

"I did skin it quick. I just used *my* knife, that's all," Lizzy protested. "Yours was all rusty." The women weren't listening. Lizzy raised her voice. "My knife is sharp."

"Now, now," Madam Cornelia said, leaning over to stroke Cook's ankle, "you know very well they haven't hung a witch in Leiden since you were a girl."

"That's as may be," Cook told her, "but it's time they started again." She groaned, much too loud.

"Shush," Madam Cornelia told her. "It will be all right. How was it you happened to fall?"

"Well, that's it, isn't it," Cook said. She pointed again at Lizzy. "It was her that tripped me. I was just making my way to the coop to fetch some eggs when that witch slunk out the kitchen door. But not as herself, oh, no. She's sneakier than that. She crept out as a cat. She'd turned herself into a witch cat, pitch-black like her filthy hair."

Lizzy's scalp began to tingle. As she ran her fingers through her hair, her cap fell back and her tangled black braids dropped loose to her shoulders.

"That cat had a bloody red mouth," Cook went on, "and eyes that were scum green like hers." The two women stared at Lizzy.

Lizzy closed her eyes. They *were* green. There was nothing she could do to change it.

"What that Devil cat did was set herself right in my path," said Cook, her voice rising again, "and then she twined round my leg, unnatural, and gave my whole weak body a witch's curse so I'd trip and fall and hurt myself almost mortal."

"Please," Lizzy said, "I'm a good Christian girl, I am. I—"

Madam Cornelia rose. "You have greatly displeased Cook, who is my treasure."

"But madam." Lizzy steadied her voice. "That same black cat was in the mill yard yesterday chasing its tail. Surely you've seen it."

Cook shrieked again, as though in fresh pain. Then she pointed once more at Lizzy. "When that witch appeared, the black cat went up in a puff of smoke. Don't you see? The witch turned herself into a cat and now she's turned herself back. The Devil helped her do it." She smiled, pleased with the story.

What if Madam Cornelia thought this was true? Lizzy gathered up her skirt, ready to run. Neither of these women could catch her. But the mill yard was filled with workers. All Madam Cornelia would have to do would be to call, "Stop that girl!" or, worse, "Stop that witch!" and someone would grab her. Running would never work.

Then, quite suddenly, the boy appeared at the door of the kitchen, followed by a heavy, ruddy man whose hair, eyebrows, and shoulders were dusted with flour. Almost certainly by the look of him, this was the miller, Harmen Gerritzen, the boy's father.

Cook began another crescendo of screaming.

"I searched the house for you, madam," he exclaimed to his wife, "to tell you that your son is a truant! He has strayed once again from the straight and narrow. Instead of attending school this morning, he went to In the Printery, that printing shop across from the Eel Market, where my friend Frans spotted him and reported it to me. I have wasted my time collecting him. Now I deliver him up to you for proper punishment."

"I'm sorry for your trouble, Sir my father," said the boy, not looking the least bit sorry. "But I already know how to read and write well enough. They were engraving a map of Paradise at the printers'. I wanted to see where the

Garden of Eden is located. It's near the Persian Sea. Do you know where Paradise is, Sir my father?"

His father shook his head and sighed. "How *are* we going to tame this child?" he asked.

"Besides," the boy went on, "I needed to watch the engravers. I think they're really very good." He looked down at the cook on the ground, chickens pecking around her. "Why is Cook sitting in the dirt?" he asked.

"Why indeed?" His father prodded Cook with his foot. "Get up, woman, there's food to be fixed. Can't go sitting about on the ground, howling."

"It's that girl," Cook whimpered. "That witch. She turned herself into a black cat and tripped me, and my ankle's broke for sure and I'll be needing crutches."

"Lizzy?" the boy asked, grinning. "A witch? Surely that's not true. Look at the mess her hair is. I think a witch would make herself tidier. Didn't you like the cookies I told her to bring you?" he asked Cook.

Cook brushed the question aside. "I have proof," she cried. "The girl used her claws to skin a hare, and then she went poof into the air when the cat appeared. She and that cat are one and the same."

"Then why doesn't she disappear right now and scat?" the boy asked, smiling. "I would. Do it for us, Lizzy. Turn into a cat. Here, kitty, kitty, kitty."

At that, the big black cat appeared in the doorway, the

leg of a neatly skinned and well-larded headless hare in her teeth. She must have dragged it down from the table and across the tile floor. Now she walked over to the boy, set the hare down at his feet, looked up at him with glinting green eyes, and meowed.

Lizzy dashed to scoop up the hare. Cradling the meat under her arm, she pointed at the cat. "See! There it is," she told them. "We can't be the same. I'm here and—" The cat fled.

"Has anyone seen Lizzy fly through the air yet?" the boy asked, laughing.

He wouldn't tell them about her jump from the windmill, would he? Lizzy dropped the hare into Cook's arms, then reached into the bag at her waist. She fingered the greasy handle of her knife and pulled it out. "*This* is what I cleaned the hare with." Pointing it a little too close to the boy's nose, she said, "It's sharper than any cat's claws."

The boy stepped back. "Well, that's that," he told them. "Anybody here still thinks Lizzy's a witch, raise your hand."

"Nonsense!" The miller laughed. "Only balmy old wives believe in witches!"

Cook sat on the ground, glowering, hugging the hare. "I want to go to my good daughter's house," she snuffled. "I know *she* ain't no child of the Devil. She'll bind up my leg like the good, loving, God-fearing girl she is."

"Poor Cook," the boy said. "Let's get two or three of Father's millers to load her in a wheelbarrow and push her to her daughter's house. It isn't far, is it?"

"But the hare," Madam Cornelia protested.

"Oh, I'll wash the dirt off with a cup of vinegar," Lizzy told them. With a huge sigh of relief, she picked up the larded meat from Cook's lap and headed for the kitchen. "It'll be as good as new."

"Nooooo," wailed the cook. "I don't want no witch near my cooking pots."

"Hush," said Master Gerritzen. "Calm down, Gertrude. I can't spare a miller to do it. But you're absolutely right. Your daughter's house is the best place for you to do your moaning."

He put his hand on the boy's shoulder. "Seeing as you have no stomach for school, young man, *you* can wheel her home. The girl can go with him," he went on, glancing at Cook with a wicked smile, "to make sure the lad comes straight back home."

Cook put her head in her hands.

"Now, you obey your loving daughter, Gertrude, and you'll come back good as new." He sighed. "Filled with your usual cheer and high spirits."

The boy bowed to his father. "Sir my father," he said, placing his hand over his heart, "I promise that tomorrow I will not only *go* to school, I will stay there all day long, learning; and at night I will read to you and to Madam my mother the story of the Prodigal Son. In Latin."

His father smiled. "A hollow promise," he told the boy. "You know perfectly well that tomorrow is Sunday, and that after church we'll be spending the whole day at the fair."

Chapter Twelve

"**I**F THAT WITCH PUTS a spell on your supper, it'll be your fault, not mine," Cook told the miller as he and the boy raised her into the wheelbarrow. When the miller just laughed, she clenched her jaws, held on tight, and braced herself for the ride.

They started off at an easy pace. "Careful," Lizzy warned the boy. "Cook did bruise her foot. It's all purple and yellow."

"A purple Cook's foot!" The boy made a face. "It sounds like the freak show. Have you ever seen a pig with two heads?" he asked Lizzy. "I never have. Ever. There's going to be one at the fair tomorrow. And dancing bears. And those really good jugglers who throw plates in the air.

You've seen them. They're at fairs a lot. I wish I could juggle. Can you?"

"You shouldn't go to the fair tomorrow, no matter what's there. Don't you know that?" she asked him. "You should honor the Sabbath. You should keep it holy."

"Slow down, you wretched children!" Cook cried out. "You'll break every good bone I have left."

Lizzy slowed. But the boy tried to speed up, and the wheelbarrow tilted dangerously toward the canal. When they stopped to right it, Lizzy whispered to the boy, "Ease up. Please. I don't want her to hate me more than she already does. I want your mother to keep me on."

The boy grinned and nodded. "I saved your life, you know," he told her. "Cook would have tied your thumbs to your big toes and tossed you in the river to see if you'd float."

"You made fun of me," Lizzy said.

He shrugged. "I just made fun because it was funny, that's all."

Pushing the wheelbarrow at a gentle roll, they passed the brand-new City Timber Wharf, its red-and-white shutters bright in the morning sun. Sailors from a two-masted boat were unloading huge oak beams, most likely from the far Baltic. The carpenters would use them in new houses going up outside the city walls. The air smelled sweet of the fresh wood.

While no amount of care could stop the bumps altogether, they eased Cook down cobblestone streets and across bridges as gently as they could. The rows of buildings on either side of the canals reflected in the water, rippling in its mirror. Cook shouted out directions as they headed toward the house where her daughter lived.

"Hold fast a minute," Lizzy said, stopping the wheelbarrow.

"Hurry *up!*" Cook called back. "Don't dawdle so. My foot needs tending."

"Truly," Lizzy said. "But I just saw a good solid pat of horse manure." She picked it up carefully and laid it next to Cook. "Your daughter'll make a fine poultice for your ankle from it. Then that foot won't swell up on you like a pig's bladder."

Cook knew how a good poultice would help, but she snorted and told them to move on.

"I know what, Cook," the boy teased. "If we stop again, Lizzy could fix you up good as new with one of her magic spells."

Cook growled and clung to the sides of the wheelbarrow with both hands. "You're a spoiled pup, young man. You'll come to no good end. And you can put that down on the fine paper you scratch around on. In Latin, if you ever learn it. *Come to no good!* The mistress and the master ought to be ashamed, letting you run so wild. And as for you, miss, if you can skin that hare as fast as an onion, then you can stop poking along and get me home."

They hurried past a rat catcher going their way, counting five especially fat dead rats dangling from the basket on his high pole. This showed how good his arsenic cake was. Ringing his bell, a milkman up ahead called out, "Milk, sweet warm milk, beautiful milk." Lizzy recognized an Englishman from the Separatist group, a clay pipe maker, coming toward them and greeted him with a short-breathed "Good day."

Creeping now through a crowd of shoppers, they edged around an old woman selling tallow candles from her cart, turned the corner at Cook's command, and stopped at the sight of her daughter sitting on a bench in front of her two-room house, shelling peas. She looked up and sighed. The toddler at her side cried out and ran to its grandmother, but Cook's daughter reeled the child back by the long cords tied at its waist.

"Fixing to kill me," Cook grumbled to her daughter as Lizzy and the boy slid her out of the wheelbarrow and onto the bench. "Brats, they are, worse than brats."

Lizzy and the boy greeted Cook's daughter, placed the pat of manure by the door, and waved a cheerful goodbye. Only the toddler waved back. Once around the corner again, they stopped. Lizzy wiped her sweaty palms on her apron. "I'd best hurry back," she told the boy. "I've got to see to the hare, chop some onions and cabbage, and do some churning. No need to make an apple tart, at least, since we've got cookies now. It'll be a good supper."

"You can't go back yet," the boy told her. He lowered his voice. "I need to show you something. It's important."

"Is it about Master Brewster?" she asked, alarmed.

He nodded. "And I think we'd better hurry," he told her. "Just now at the printers, when my father caught me, I was in all truth watching the engravers, but that's not all. I just happened to look outside, and I could see those two men from yesterday. They were across the canal, eating herring and pretzels, like that's all they had to do, but they had their eyes glued on the printers' shop. I think they know that's where those pamphlets were printed. They're still looking for your Brewster. Anybody could see what they were up to. They are really stupid spies."

This was a terrible day. Before today, she'd never ever heard of Englishmen looking for Master Brewster in Leiden. Now she'd heard it twice. But each time, it was only the boy who'd said it. And he had, after all, tricked her onto the windmill.

Lizzy turned his chin so he'd have to look her straight in the eye. "You're not making this up, are you?" she asked.

"I *said* I wasn't." He stuck out his lip, annoyed. Shaking his chin free, he picked up a handle of the wheelbarrow

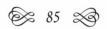

and started to push. "You warned him, didn't you?"

Lizzy grabbed her handle and followed his lead. "He wasn't home. I told Mistress Brewster what you told me. His daughter Patience went looking for him. But maybe she didn't find him. You think he's been at the printers' and they've captured him?" Had she failed Master Brewster?

"Haven't done," the boy said. "Unless they're hanging about looking for somebody else." He pointed down the road to two men standing in front of Blaeus' bakery. "See them?" the boy went on. "That fellow in the scarlet doublet and that one in the purple with those yellow insets in his breeches. If I was a spy, I'd wear black so nobody would notice me, wouldn't you?"

He pointed the wheelbarrow straight at the men in purple and scarlet. "Shall we run them over by mistake and knock them in the canal, where they'll drown dead?" he asked. "I bet they can't swim. I can't. Can you by now?"

"Thou shalt not kill," Lizzy told him, not sure if he had meant it. "Anyway, running them down would just make them mad as bees. Maybe I should go looking for Master Brewster again."

"No, then I'd have no supper. I've got an idea," the boy said, stopping. "You tell the men you know where this Brewster is. Tell them he went back to England or—I don't know—America. Only not here. Then they'll go away and search someplace else. Otherwise, they're just going to hang around here until they find him, don't you think? Isn't that what spies do?"

Lizzy didn't want to lie to these strange men. She didn't want to say anything to them. Still, the boy might be right. If the spies could prove that Master Brewster had written something against the English law, maybe the Dutch really would let them tie up his hands and take him back to England. If she could just tell these men something to make them go away, then Master Brewster might be out of danger.

"Wait," she said, trying to think what she would say, but the boy kept the wheelbarrow rolling almost to the toes of the fancy-dressed men, whose heads stuck out of their wide collars like ruffled pink tulips.

"Good day, fine sirs," said the boy politely, bowing to each man.

Lizzy stared at their feet. They both wore striped silk stockings and satin ribbons tied in huge bows to fasten their shoes.

"Yesterday," the boy went on, "I heard you ask questions about an Englishman. I brought you somebody who knows where he is. And for twenty duiten, she'll tell you what she knows."

They scarcely moved. Their starched lace collars were matched by cuffs just as wide and stiff. They held their

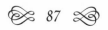

87

heads high and looked down their noses.

The man in purple glanced back and forth from Lizzy to the boy, frowned, then remembered. "Oh, it's the silly lad who thought red wine would wash off treasonous words. Charming child." He patted the boy on the head. "But of course we would be willing to reward anyone who helps us find our . . . friend." He covered his smile with yellow gloves.

The boy stiffened at the man's touch, but he nodded. "Yes, me. This is my friend. Her name is Lizzy."

The man in the scarlet doublet, which was trimmed in wide gold braid, smiled broadly. "Well. Lizzy, is it? Elizabeth. A good English name. Where are you from, my dear?"

"Scrooby, sir," she said in a small voice. "In Nottinghamshire, sir."

"Well, then," he went on, "you must know the Brewsters. They're from Scrooby, as well. Fine family."

"I know them," she said weakly.

"No need to be afraid, my dear," the man went on, his words oily with kindness. "It's only William Brewster we seek, not his wife and babes, or," and he laughed at the foolishness of the thought, "you."

"First, the twenty duiten," the boy told them. "Then she'll tell you what she knows, won't you, Lizzy?"

"Oh, no, I can't, I—" This was too hard. She couldn't do it.

"Ten duiten, and only if you're quick about it," the man in the purple doublet said sharply.

"Ten's enough. Go ahead, tell him!" The boy nudged her with his elbow.

Lizzy didn't know what to tell. This had happened too fast. They had swords at their sides. If the knife in my pocket was a sword, she thought desperately, I'd just draw it out and, instead of lying, I'd tell them how I'd cut them to bits like eels and I'd scare them far away. But it wasn't a sword and she was the one who was scared, so she stood with her mouth shut, her skin prickling with fear.

"You'd like to go back to England, wouldn't you, little miss? You want to go back to those rolling green hills where they speak the King's English instead of this guttural garbage, don't you? When was the last time you ate a chunk of rich, fat beef with Yorkshire pudding? Tastes like manna. Remember? And you still love your good King James, don't you, my sweet?" He cupped her chin in his hand. She shook it free. "If you like, we'll take you back," he went on. "We could take you back—free of charge." His smile oozed sincerity.

Lizzy glanced across the canal in panic, trying to think how to make these men go away. What she saw there made her heart jump, but she held her breath steady. Walking briskly down the street was a short man with a trim gray mustache and goatee. His doublet was forest green, his cap brown leather. She looked away as he opened the door of the printing shop and stepped inside. It was Master Brewster.

"You know where he is, don't you?" said the man in scarlet.

She knew exactly where he was: He was just a bridge away. The door of In the Printery slammed shut. She knew at once what she had to do.

Lizzy smiled her biggest smile, brighter and even less sincere than the spies'. She held out her palm to the man in the rich purple doublet. "Ten duiten, please," she said.

Chapter Thirteen

*L*IZZY COULD FEEL the red in her cheeks. Did it make her look guilty? She took a deep breath.

"I don't know if I should tell you this," she began. "Are you good men and true?"

"Here's the money," the man in the purple doublet said, slapping the coins into Lizzy's open hand. "Now, where can we find him?"

Lizzy curled her fingers and made a fist around the coins, digging their edges into her palm. She moved closer to the bakery, drawing the men's eyes away from the printers' shop across the canal.

"It's . . . it's at least two, three days since they left," she said, as if this was a mighty secret and they were pulling it out of her like a rotten tooth. "The whole lot of them packed up." She waited to decide what to say. "They took themselves off . . . to Amsterdam. That's a place we stopped for some months when we first came to Holland."

"They did stay in Amsterdam, almost a year," the scarlet spy told the purple one. "But they've gone back there, you say?" he asked Lizzy. "Why would they do that? You're absolutely sure?"

"Yes, sir," she told him, nodding. "There was some argument among the men." Now that she'd started to lie, she had to make it sound like truth. "He took the whole family with him—his wife, Mary; and then Jonathan and his wife; and Patience, Fear, Love, and the baby, Wrestling."

"Those are the names," the purple spy said. "Who'd forget them? That's our man."

The boy had picked up a long, stout stick and was drawing in the dirt.

"I don't believe you," the scarlet spy said. He grabbed her wrist tightly, and twisted.

Lizzy gasped, and, dipping her knee as if in a curtsy, she tried to wrest her arm free. She raised her chin and looked him straight in the eye. "Lying is a sin, sir," she said slowly.

"They went back to Amsterdam," she went on, "to join up with the Ancient Brethren. That's the congregation there. Their old minister, Master Clyfton, is still in Amsterdam. I thought, sir, they were your friends and you wanted to see them, and so I told you."

Lizzy's stomach churned as she watched the boy out of the corner of her eye. He was edging closer to the men, holding his stick with both hands like a club. He'd better not try it, Lizzy thought. They'd slice him in two.

"Well," said the scarlet spy, shrugging, "it's all we've got. We'll try Amsterdam." He gave her wrist another sharp twist. "But, little miss, your king has ways to find you out, the way he found out who printed your treasonous William Brewster's words." He raised his voice. "The king is your mighty lord and sovereign, no matter where you live."

"Please, sir, my wrist," Lizzy shouted out, trying to pry his hand from her arm.

He looked at her closely, searching out the lie. "You had better not be wrong," he told her.

"Wrong? Is something wrong?" Jan, hearing the noise, had stepped out of the bakery, clapping the flour from his hands. At once, the scarlet spy dropped Lizzy's arm, flicked a perfumed handkerchief out of his pocket, and rubbed his fingers with it as though to clean away her touch.

Jan reached back and lifted the sheep horn off its hook near the bakery door. Lizzy stepped toward him. "These men hurting you, Lizzy?" he asked. "Shall I sound an alarm?"

The two spies rested their hands on the hilts of their

swords and bowed deeply, mocking them. Then they turned and began to saunter away.

Lizzy's knees were shaking. She wanted those men well gone before Master Brewster walked out of the printers' shop. She grabbed the horn from Jan's hand, pressed it to her lips, and pointed it straight at the men. Calling up all the breath her lungs could hold, she blew one loud trumpeting blast and then another and another. The spies must have thought it was, at the least, a Dutch call to arms. Swords clanking, they scurried away.

"Thank you," Lizzy said, handing the horn to Jan. "They needed scaring."

"Nothing to thank me for," Jan told her, holding his ears and laughing. "You were just blowing the bread horn is all. It was time. Fresh bread!" he called across the canal. "Hot from the oven. Fresh rye bread. Get it while it's hot!" And he blew the horn again.

The boy threw down his stick. "You probably couldn't tell it," he told Jan, "but those men were spies."

Jan laughed. "And what big secrets do you know?"

Lizzy wanted to tell him. She felt almost proud now that she'd deceived them, had done it without flinching. She wanted to hear Jan say, "Now, *that* was a lie worth telling." But what if he thought it wasn't? She didn't want Jan ever to think ill of her. So she just opened her hand to him and held out the coins.

"Here's nine duiten for this morning's cookies," Lizzy said, handing him all the money. "And with what's left, we'll have a pretzel to share, the boy and me."

Jan lifted not one but two fresh hot pretzels from the holder that hung outside the bakery door. "Quick payment," he told her, with a smile she couldn't help answer.

"I'll come soon with the cloth you loaned me," she said, and waved him good-bye.

Lizzy knew they must hurry, but her knees felt weak. As she and the boy pushed the wheelbarrow back toward the mill, Lizzy glanced behind her. "Are they following us, do you think?" she asked him. Her voice was still unsteady.

"Not unless they've changed into gray and brown with shell buttons," he said, stopping to rest. "I'll see about getting the cookie money from Madam my mother," he told her. "But you owe me five duiten from the spy's ten."

"Five! You didn't do anything but scratch the ground with a stick."

"Asking for money was my idea. I should get *more* than five. I should get seven. I need more sticks of chalk."

She knew she shouldn't keep any. It was dirty money. What would Papa have thought of her, taking money for lying? "I don't want it," she told the boy. "When I get paid back for the cookies, you can have it, every duit."

As they rolled along, he asked her, "How did you pay to get here from England, anyway? You're poor as a mouse.

Poorer, I bet, since you won't take money that falls in your lap."

"We didn't pay. Papa didn't have money to spare," she told him. "Hop in the wheelbarrow. I'll give you a ride. It's easier with one person pushing, anyway." The boy climbed in, lay back, and folded his hands behind his head. She started off slowly.

"It was Master Brewster's money paid for us all to come," she began. "It was no great hardship for him. He had lots of money then, got it when his rich father died. Most of it's gone by now, I expect. First big lot of it went when he hired a boat to carry us to Amsterdam. It was late that same fall when I got sick from jumping in the moat. Remember, I told you?

"Papa had married Sally by then. She made me a doll. She made it from a whole sleeve of red wool, most likely ripped out in a fight. Someone had left it behind in one of the rooms at the manor house.

"I named the doll Hannah. After my mother. How I loved my new doll. Sally made her as long as my arm was then and wrapped her tight like a newborn swaddling baby. She stuffed her with lamb's wool to make her soft, and tied her up with ribbon. A bit of white sheeting made her face. With tiny stitches, she made two big eyes, a nose, and a mouth that went straight across. No smile."

"I don't want to hear about any doll," the boy called

from the wheelbarrow bed. He was still chewing on his pretzel. "Am I too heavy?"

"No, you're fine," she said, though her shoulders ached. "The doll is part of the story. You have to hear about Hannah. Later, she gets to hold a treasure.

"Well, when Master Brewster decided we had to leave England, he paid a huge lot of money to an English sea captain to take us across to Amsterdam. He had to give him more than he should have because, of course, our going to Holland was against the law."

"That's called a bribe," the boy said. "I've heard of bribes."

"But he had to do it," Lizzy went on. "The king didn't want his subjects sneaking out. He wanted us to stay there under his thumb. So we sold all we could and packed up only what was truly needful. But Sally and Papa let me keep Hannah. She didn't take much room, I hugged her so close all the way.

"We got ourselves from Scrooby to the seashore, some by horse, some by foot, and Sally and me packed in with all the women and children floating in a barge. We got to this town called Boston, in Lincolnshire, right on the dot of when that captain said he'd meet us. But he wasn't there.

"We waited for two whole days and nights, on the ready to board the ship, trying to look like we belonged there.

It wasn't till late the second night that the captain came into port. And then he herded us on board fast with all our trunks and bundles. It was the dark of night, but we could tell the boat was rickety. We could hear it creak. All of us were wary, not just the little ones. And we were right to be.

"We'd hardly sailed out of the harbor when men-at-arms poured out of the hold like a pack of rats and swarmed over the deck. They pointed their guns at us and flashed their knives and told us to hand over everything we had. They said they were officers of the law. You see, that captain had taken Master Brewster's money and then turned us in. He got a reward for it, too. Got paid twice."

"What did you do?" the boy asked. "Did you toss the men overboard and sail the boat yourselves? I expect that's how you got here."

"Well, not hardly," Lizzy scoffed. "You don't toss men overboard when they've got drawn daggers. And guns. They could blow your head off. They could do what they wanted, couldn't they? They tore all our things from us— money, good pewter plates, knives, spoons, our Bibles even. They were searching us to the skin, even the women, in ways that weren't modest.

"Papa had his fists up, ready to smack any of them that went for Sally, when Master Brewster came up behind him. He snuck a packet in Papa's hand and said, 'Hide this, Goodman Tinker, if you can. It's what money we have left. They'd find it on me for certain.' Then Master Brewster, he stepped forward and he and young William Bradford, who was about eighteen at the time, they started an argument with the officers.

"It turned into a big ruckus, with some of the other Scrooby men joining in. My friend Will's father got his arm cut up pretty bad in the fight.

"Papa said he was just testing his brains, trying to think what to do with all that money, when he looked down and there I was, clinging to his leg, with Hannah pressed to my chest. He whispered something to Sally, then left us to join in the fight.

"Sally pulled me over to a dark place where a big rope was coiled, sat me down on it, took Hannah, and pulled out all her wool stuffing. I knew better than to cry. Then she filled the doll back up quick with that roll of money.

"'Hug her tight, Lizzy,' Sally said, giving the doll back to me. 'Hug her tight as a tick.'

"After a time, the fighting over, they started pushing the lot of us out onto little open boats and rowing us back to shore. When I tripped getting out, one of them tried to grab my Hannah away, but I clung to that doll. I kicked him in the shins and ran."

Lizzy paused and looked up, to see two familiar windmills ahead. "Are you asleep?" she asked the boy. "We're home."

 99

"Of course I'm not asleep," he said, climbing out of the wheelbarrow. "I don't understand that story. I thought you were going to tell me how you got here. After all that, you didn't even end up in Holland."

"Not then," Lizzy said. "They marched us into town, and, night or not, the townspeople all flocked out and poked fun at us. They locked most of the men up in jail. Next day, they made the women and children go back to Scrooby, which wasn't even home to us anymore."

"Lizzy! You, girl! Lizzy!" Madam Cornelia called from the house. "The hare's almost done. There's work to do. Come along now. What took you so long? Poor Lysbet is all tired out from turning the spit. How's Cook?"

The boy stretched. "What happened to Hannah?"

Lizzy laughed. "She wasn't so soft with the lamb's wool gone. But I slept with her close anyway, and her new insides went to good use. A few months later, they went to pay the next sea captain."

When Lizzy entered the kitchen, the black cat ran in from the garden and rubbed against her leg. It stayed at her feet, purring as she chopped and sliced and stirred for supper. It was a fine meal the miller's family would be having that night.

"Cat," Lizzy said, rubbing its neck, "you're a good creature. And Cook said you were me." When the cat meowed, Lizzy laughed out loud. It seemed funny now,

but it hadn't then. It might not be so bad to be a cat, Lizzy thought, just slinking in and out, eating bits of sweet meat from the spit, not wondering about right and wrong.

At the Brewsters' that night, Lizzy said nothing about being called a witch. She did tell Master Brewster about the men dressed in scarlet and purple and what they'd said to her. He did not mention that what she'd said was a lie. He frowned as he listened, but told her it was not her worry.

Still, before she climbed on the mattress with Fear and Patience, she took a worn red doll out of her clothes bundle and carried it, and the worry, to bed.

Chapter Fourteen

"YOU KNOW WHAT I heard?" Lizzy asked Will. "I heard there'll be a real live dancing bear at the fair today. And a pig with two heads. We could never go, of course, because that would be dishonoring the Sabbath. But there'll be a clown there called Pekelharing. And Gypsies who can tell your fortune. At least, that's what the little boy from the Gerritzen place said. I warned him he shouldn't go either, but he will. He wouldn't miss it. He's not a bad little boy really. He's the one who warned me about the spies. Oh, Will, do you think they might find Master Brewster and capture him?"

Lizzy stopped to glance up at Will. He wasn't listening. She could tell. He had been waiting for her at the end of Stink Alley. Now he trudged along beside her, twisting his old brown cap in his hands. She studied his face. He looked the same, but there was a strangeness about him.

They were on their way to the Green Close for Sunday-morning Meeting. The Green Close was a large house fronting St. Peter's Square that was owned by the Separatists. Pastor John Robinson and his wife lived upstairs, and his congregation met for their services in a large room downstairs. Every Sunday morning, Meeting went from eight to noon. First they prayed together. Then they stood and sang in unison. Then they listened to Pastor Robinson's sermon, three hours or more.

The women sat on one side of the aisle, men on the other. The children sat in back, quietly. If they whined or fretted, a deaconess with a birch switch snapped them into quiet.

Then every Sunday, they went to afternoon Meeting. It lasted until dark. That's when the men of the congregation did something that in England they could have been arrested for. They talked about what the Bible meant. In England, the ministers told *them*.

The pattern was always the same although in summer the daylight and the Meetings lasted longer. Never on the Sabbath did the women cook. Never did the children play. Never would any of them go to a Sunday fair. That would have been clearly sinful.

Though the Green Close meeting place was only a

short way from the Brewsters' Stink Alley home, the family had left for Meeting before first light, looking left and right and into the shadows, careful to see that no one was watching.

Lizzy had left later. When she'd stepped out of Stink Alley, she had checked the doorways carefully, though the spies did not look to her like early risers. They would, most like, still be abed at the inn called The Sandwich Arms, where Englishmen often stayed.

No spies were at the corner, but Will was. "I want to talk to you," he'd said urgently, but then he hadn't talked at all. When Lizzy told him about the danger, he'd barely nodded. They'd walked twice around St. Peter's Square, and still he was silent.

The September air was warm and damp. Taking a deep breath, Lizzy frowned. Then she smiled, hoping to cheer him. "I know how you've changed, Will," she said. "You smell sweet today."

His face reddened. "Mum gave my clothes a good wash," he told her. "I asked her to. She put some mint in the rinse, and"—he lowered his head—"I took a bath. It doesn't seem to have hurt me. Yet." Baths were rare things. They used up good water, and besides, they were unhealthy. It was a known fact.

St. Peter's Square was beginning to bustle with people, most on their way to the church for services, some few still hurrying to the Green Close for Meeting. Will drew Lizzy aside into the doorway of the corner bookstore. He bent his head toward her ear. "Lizzy-bit, I have something I must tell you," he began, his eyes scared. "Everyone, I fear, will be mad at me and John for it. I know they will. It's a terrible secret, but you've got to promise, sacred word, you won't let on. Not till after Meeting."

Were they going to skip Meeting and go to the fair? They wouldn't. Couldn't. Had John fallen in with bad company? She'd heard it said. That would be grim. How could she keep such a thing quiet?

"Promise?" he asked her. Will's eyes were sad and pleading. Lizzy nodded solemnly. Glancing toward the Green Close, she asked, "Where *is* John?"

"Waiting for me on Old Castle Hill." He rubbed his forehead as if it hurt. "Listen," he whispered, "we've thought a lot about this, John and me. And we're leaving."

She opened her mouth to protest.

"No, don't stop me. I want to tell you. We're going to sea. Maybe we'll go to the Indies. Or Brazil."

"Brazil?" Nobody went to Brazil. He was teasing. Surely. She laughed. "Oh, Will, in truth, you are not," she said, and, smiling, she gave him a shove with her shoulder.

"In all truth, we are," he told her, shaking his head. "John and me both, we've had it up to here with the reek of that wool and never seeing the sun shine. It is like the plague to us. We'd die of it." He straightened up tall. "We both washed ourselves, if you want to know, because we didn't want to take our stench along. John and me, we want to see the world. I bet we see pigs with *three* heads. And bears. And lions and tigers and whales."

Lions and tigers! This was too much. Lizzy laughed again. Why, he was just talking big. The laughter caught in her throat, though, when he would not laugh back. He meant it. But he couldn't go. It was wrong. It was sinfully wrong. There were words in the Bible that told him not to. She closed her eyes to call them up. "'It is good for a man that he bear the yoke in his youth,'" she told him. "From Lamentations. Remember? It means we're *meant* to work hard. You and me both. And John, too."

"I don't mind work. You know I don't, but we're rotting in those fulling tubs," Will said, shaking his head. "'A prudent man seeth the plague, and hideth himself,'" he quoted.

The vats are not the plague truly, Lizzy thought, but it is true that Will has sickened from them. If he stays, his skin will stink forever. His back will be forever bowed. Can that be God's will? Is he wrong to want to escape?

She tried to hold herself calm. "They won't take you on. You're just twelve years old. That's not old enough. Can't be."

A family walking by greeted them. Mechanically, they

both smiled, nodded, and said, "Good morning."

Will turned back to her. "Already *have* taken me, haven't they? Told them I was sixteen. John said he was eighteen. We're tall. And we're signed up. John made his X and I signed my name full. We're going."

Lizzy felt her throat lock. It was done? They'd signed their names? "But—but Pastor Robinson, Master Brewster—your *parents!*" Lizzy raised her voice. "They're going to think Satan called you."

"Quiet," he told her, taking her hand. "You promised."

"Oh, Will, don't go. Who would I talk to? Who would listen? You stay here and you'll be an elder when you grow up. You heard Master Brewster say it. You'll lead us in the paths of righteousness."

"We're away," Will said, pulling his hand back and putting on his brown cap. "Don't you see? I don't want to be like William Brewster. All rigid. Ever stern with my children. Not able to show them love like I see the Dutch do. That's what I *don't* want. My brother and me, we're setting our own path. It's righteous, too. We don't need William Brewster or Pastor Robinson to help us pray true. And that's that."

His voice softened. "Please, Lizzy, Mum and Pa don't know. Pa always said we were turning into old men before his eyes, so he'll understand. But we didn't tell them. We were afraid it would go hard on them with the congregation if they knew and didn't stop us. I think they'll miss us with all their hearts." He reached out and touched her cheek. "In faith, Lizzy, you understand, don't you?"

"No. Yes. No." She didn't want him to leave. Yet, it may be she understood. Some. When she thought of Papa's loving night tales, when she thought of all the laughing at little Jacob's breeching, even when she thought of the funny miller's boy, spoiled by his parents, she knew she'd want to give her children that kind of love. But she'd always thought they'd be her children and Will's. He was her Will.

"Lizzy, John said I shouldn't tell you, but I didn't want just to disappear. I want you to know why we're going and I want you to explain to Mum and Pa the things I told you. They'll understand. They love you. Go to them after and comfort them. Please."

"Will." Her head was spinning. "How can I? What will I say?" she asked, her voice shaking. "Are you never coming back?" Could this be happening? How could she stop him?

He wiped his eyes.

"Wait." She tugged at the sleeve of his doublet. "Go get John and bring him back. You're not sailors and you know it. After that crossing *we* had, how could you think the sea would be better than here with us? Remember that storm? How could you forget? You were sick every day. I thought we were going to die. *You* thought we were going to die."

"Well, we didn't," Will said. "So John and me, we're going to live a real life. Out in the sun." He looked her hard in the eyes. "You promised me, Lizzy. Wait till after Meeting. At noon, we join some of John's friends on the Corn Market bridge. Soon after, the lot of us will be out the city gates and well on our way to Amsterdam.

"What you can tell Mum and Pa is that we've gone to sea, that we didn't just run off to nowhere. You can tell them that. It'll be hard on them both, though I think Pa suspects." He was looking over his shoulder now, tightening up like a coil ready to spring. "Lizzy, help Mum and Pa. Go and sit with them at home. At the end of the day, talk to them in English. Tell them we said we love them and wish them God's blessing."

He turned quickly down Choir Alley but then ran back. Lifting Lizzy off the ground, he gave her a short, awkward hug. Then, this time without stopping, he headed off to Old Castle Hill, where his brother, John, would be waiting. And then to Amsterdam and the sea.

"Godspeed," she whispered. She tasted the salt in her mouth before she knew she was crying. Had she failed him? Brushing her cheeks dry, Lizzy walked to the Green Close by herself. Bells rang out from St. Peter's tower. It was eight o'clock. She was late.

When she opened the door, all she had to do was shout, "Will and John are running away! They're in Satan's power. You can save them at Old Castle Hill!" It was, of course, forbidden for women to speak aloud in Meeting, but they'd forgive her this. If Pastor Robinson and Master Brewster were right, it was her duty to cry out. But then, Will had said they were not always right.

Inside the Green Close, the air was dense with heat and quiet. Lizzy studied the rows of bowed heads. If I shouted out the news, the men would scatter like ants, she thought. Will's parents would be stricken. The women would hug their arms tightly around themselves, afraid of the loss. The babies, aware of the stir, would cry.

Was it God's will or Satan that made them leave? She had to decide for herself. Lizzy took a deep breath. She would put her trust in Will and hope that this was truly God's plan for him. She had given him her word. She kept the quiet.

Patience Brewster frowned her disapproval as Lizzy slipped in beside her, trembling. Pastor Robinson raised his voice. The prayers had begun.

Chapter Fifteen

*D*URING PRAYERS, Lizzy's thoughts would not leave Will. They had lived their whole lives—twelve years—together, as if in the same entwining tale. Now he was starting a fresh trail, which she could only imagine. She wanted to stop him. Already he would be racing up the grassy mound of Old Castle Hill. The castle fort sat so high on the hill, you could see all of Leiden at the top. Even if she'd sent the men, Will and John would have seen them coming. They'd have run and escaped catching.

As they sang psalms together, Lizzy mouthed the words, but questions kept filling her head. Would the boys take the ferry across the Braassemer lake, or save money and walk the long marsh-lined road to Amsterdam? Might they be tempted to break their morning fast to eat hot sugared pancakes at the fair? Might they have their fortunes told by a Gypsy? What if the Gypsy said to beware of the future? What was their future?

Then Lizzy's back straightened with a new thought. She hoped suddenly against hope that what she'd said had turned Will around. She turned to stare at the door. Maybe, just maybe, they were about to ease it open and come in, heads bowed. She stared at it hard, willing it to open, but the door to the Green Close stayed shut.

"And thou sayest every man for himself?" Pastor Robinson was asking in his sermon. "God never taught thee this. No, it is a position of Satan." His voice droned on and on.

But are they so bad, taking themselves away? Lizzy wondered. They're just English country lads who grew up on the farm. That's all. What is so evil in wanting to breathe free? God is in Brazil, too, surely. What, for that matter, was so evil about Papa giving her hugs and praise? Even if Master Brewster said it, Papa wasn't bad. Could it be I'm not bad, either? she wondered.

She tried to listen closely as Pastor Robinson preached, but soon she fell to her own thoughts again. Will would hate the sea. She began to think of the time she and Will had spent on the open sea. The one awful time.

What had happened was the story Papa had told her

most often at night. "Tell me," she'd beg, "the story of the crossing. Tell it again." And he'd begin. Again.

After the English captain betrayed them, some of the men had been thrown in jail. Lizzy's papa was one of them. She'd had to go back to Scrooby with Sally and the rest of the group. There, they'd talked their way into old friends' houses, but, truth to tell, most Scrooby folk hadn't wanted to be friends with enemies of the king.

Half a year later, though, the men were out of jail and they could try again to go to Amsterdam. It was in the spring of 1608. Lizzy was five and a half years old. This time, William Brewster hired a ship from a Dutch sea captain he trusted. The captain said he'd meet them on a deserted shore a good distance from any town.

So they all packed up again. The women and the small children left Scrooby on a low boat. It floated through narrow waterways and down the Idle River to an outlet on the seashore.

Papa had always laughed about how Lizzy didn't want to ride with the littlest children in the boat. He'd seemed pleased that she'd wanted to stay with him. He had told her how she'd begged him to carry her piggyback, and he couldn't say no. She was light as Sally's biscuits. The boys and men set out, some walking, a few on horseback, Lizzy sometimes running with Will, sometime riding on her father's shoulders. It was forty miles to the place where they would meet the captain.

The boat with the women and babies got there first, but the open sea was roiling. They were getting seasick, Papa had told her, and that's why the sailors pulled into a shallow creek, to calmer water. That was, he'd said, a big mistake.

The Dutch captain, though, was as good as his word. The ship came on time, and the men and boys got on at once, Lizzy with them. But the tide was out. The boat with the women and children was stuck in the mud of the emptied creek.

Papa's voice had always become excited and shaky when he'd told her what happened next. That's when the Dutch captain looked out and saw a great company of horsemen coming at them full gallop, with guns. "*Sacremente!*" he yelled. The captain didn't want to be blown out of the water or thrown in jail, but Papa had always faulted him for what happened next. The captain didn't wait for the women and little children all mired in the creek. He ordered the anchor to be raised at once.

The wind was fair then, Papa had told her. The sails filled and billowed with it. And off they went. The men stood moaning at the rails of the ship, helpless, watching the horsemen approach. There was nothing they could do. They were at sea. Their wives and children were ashore, about to be arrested.

Lizzy remembered it. She had cried for Sally and for baby Fear.

Will had sobbed, standing with Lizzy on the deck. His brother, John, clung to his father, who wept, as well. "Take us back," Will had pleaded. "I want my mum."

But they didn't go back. And it wasn't only the women and children who were left behind. Everything the men owned was packed in that boat in the mud. Papa would shake his head when he told her, "We had only the clothes on our backs. And our faith in God."

"When Job was brought to the dunghill," Pastor Robinson said, lifting his voice to the congregation, "he sat down upon it." Lizzy shook her head as if from sleep. "Thou must be content," he went on, "to receive at God's hands evil as well as good."

Evil. Lizzy took a deep breath. So much evil. We were fleeing from it, from the evil of the king. Should we have been content to stay? At the time, Papa had said, the ship itself felt evil.

Papa said it should have taken them two days to cross the Channel, but they were hit by an angry storm. Its howling winds sucked them back as much as heaved them forward. They veered so far off course that once, he'd said, they could see the coast of Norway. For the first nine days, the ship blew out of control, diving into the water, shooting into the air, almost lost in the fog. Lizzy and Will clung together belowdecks.

Everyone wept and prayed, but the roar of the sea and the creak of the boards were even louder than their prayers. Lizzy remembered the sailors crying, "We sink. We sink!" She had believed them. "Be brave, Lizzy, and strong," her papa had told her, and she had tried.

On the tenth day out, a spell of quiet fell on the sea. One of the seamen, climbing down into the hold, his oiled coat white with salt, saw Lizzy curled up behind a ladder. He knelt by her. "It's all right, poppet," he said. "We'll land you on a safe shore. Don't cry." He reached into the worn leather bag at his waist. "Here. I have a present to make you smile. It's been good luck to me. I got it in the Indies. It's a shell called a cowrie. They use it there for money." Lizzy kept her eyes down. "Here," he said. "Take it and hold on tight."

The seashell was a shiny light brown dotted with small white spots. She took it with a smile, but without a thank-you. It was too beautiful. She couldn't speak. The shell filled her fist. When the seaman left, she held its coolness against her cheek. Then she tucked it into the folds of her red-rag Hannah. The doll was soaked with the sea, but soft again, at least, with fresh lamb's wool. The money that she and Sally had stuffed in the doll had been taken out. Master Brewster had used it to buy this trip.

The seaman had been right. Four days later, they came ashore in Amsterdam, gray with sickness, purple and yellow with welts and bruises, but alive.

Lizzy raised her head. Outside the Meeting house, St. Peter's bells began to toll twelve. Pastor Robinson was speaking still. "'Mine enemies compass me round about to take away my soul,'" he said. "'They lie waiting in my way on every side, turning their eyes to the ground.'" He looked at Lizzy.

She looked away. He's talking straight to me, she thought. I turned my eyes to the ground when I let Will go. Am I, then, his enemy?

She shivered as if an icy breeze had passed. There was talk, she remembered with a start, of more war with Spain. If that happened, sailors like Will would be in the middle of it. There'd be sabers to slice him through. There'd be Spanish muskets to shoot him dead. His Dutch friends would be fighting for their country, but not Will. She didn't want him to die.

Lizzy stood up. A few heads turned. She opened her mouth to ask for help, then closed it again. She'd promised Will.

She must go by herself and somehow plead with him. She could not keep her eyes turned to the ground. She did not believe that by looking for freedom, he would lose

his soul. Will's soul was pure and safe. She was sure of that. But she was sorely afraid for his life. Patience tugged at her skirt, but Lizzy pulled away and, without looking back, fled from the Meeting.

Chapter Sixteen

THE BELLS OF SABBATH noon answered one another from churches all over Leiden. The air echoed with them. Lizzy walked briskly, stopping only when she'd gotten halfway down Choir Alley. She looked back. No one was following.

They'll think I'm sick, she decided. They'll believe that's why I left too soon. And, in faith, I am sick that Will has gone.

The noon bells were fading. The boys must be on the Corn Market bridge by now, she thought, taking long strides. They'd be talking it over, perhaps, or changing their minds, or breathing in the sweet, rich smells of the fair.

By the time she reached the town hall, the crowd was

gathering. Clumps of students from the university, singing songs in languages Lizzy couldn't understand, blocked the street, arms around one another, dancing and laughing.

Threading her way briskly through the fairgoers, Lizzy searched for Will and John. Market stalls, set up on both sides of the canal, were thick with customers. A family stood clustered at a pottery booth ahead, each child waving a coin for one of the shrill clay whistles shaped like roosters.

At a musical instrument stall in a striped fringed tent, a cluster of people were laughing at a boy who was trying to play a bagpipe, making rude, awful sounds. From the back, the boy looked very like Will. Surely Will wouldn't have stopped for such a thing. But yet, she elbowed her way closer, calling his name. The red-faced boy with the bagpipe spun around, grinning. He was just a boy, surrounded by his gleeful family. He wasn't running from anything.

Up ahead, the Corn Market bridge arched high over the canal, crowded with fairgoers. Will had said they were meeting John's friends at noon, but while there were many townspeople milling about, laughing and eating, she saw no Will or John. At the top of the arch, she had a wider view. That's when she spotted them.

Not far beyond the bridge, a tight rope stretched high over a narrow street. Carefully, one foot forward and then the other, a man in a shiny orange suit with spangles was making his way across the swaying rope, holding himself steady with a long balance pole. Will and John, shifting their feet nervously, stood below with a group of laughing boys. The boys were staring up, calling out advice: "One step to the right!" "Faster, fellow, you're being followed!" "Watch out, there's a goose going to land on your pole!"

I'll just join them slow, Lizzy thought, preparing herself. But what could she say? "Don't go; it's evil to think of yourselves!" That's what Pastor Robinson would tell them. "Don't go; you'll die!" she could say. They would never believe it.

As she stepped off the bridge, Lizzy glanced up at the balancing man and stumbled on a mottled gray dog that was sniffing out bits of fish and cheese caught in the stones. It growled and jumped at her.

"Scat!" she told it. Lifting her skirts to hurry, she pushed through the crowd toward the boys. The dog, keeping up with her, began to snap at her ankles. "Stop it!" she shouted, jumping away. "Stop it!"

John recognized her voice and turned. Lizzy could hear his raised cry. "She's here. She tattled. I knew she would. They're after us." He grabbed Will's arm and pulled him down the street by the canal, their friends following close behind.

"It's just *me!*" Lizzy shouted, going after them, the dog at her heels.

"Tell your fortune, little miss?" A woman in a purple turban stepped in front of her, fanning out a deck of cards. "Love and riches lie ahead. Tell your fortune?"

"Radishes, sweet red radishes!" A hawker waved a bunch in Lizzy's face. "Have a bite?"

For the boys, who were running as a group, the way was slow. Lizzy could still see them.

In front of her, next to the canal, a crowd was beginning to press around a juggler in a belled fool's cap. Two blue plates flew high above his head. A woman in black, his helper, tossed him another and then another, until he had four plates spinning in the air. He stood in a risky place. One misstep and he'd land in the water. His awed watchers turned quiet and moved back to give him room. They were pitching coins at his bare feet.

The boys were already at the edge of the crowd, heading toward the next bridge. Will was lagging now, yet even with his weak legs, he was well ahead of Lizzy. That small space between the juggler and his audience looked just wide enough for her to slip through and catch up. The barking dog still at her heels, she chanced it.

In a flying leap, she landed on a pile of coins, slipped on them, and fell to her knees. The dog stopped, too, right at the juggler's bare toes. It snarled and snapped. Hopping away to miss the dog's teeth, the juggler broke his rhythm and missed a plate. It shattered on the cobblestones. Then a second fell. It broke in two. The juggler swore. The woman who'd tossed the plates to him grabbed the third one just in time. He reached for the fourth, but it was too far back. He tilted toward the water. Windmilling his arms, he cried for help. The woman, hugging the plate she'd saved, screamed. As she got to her feet, Lizzy saw the juggler fall back, arms still winding. He hit the murky brown water with an enormous splash.

The audience loved it. They hooted and clapped. Lizzy turned to run. But the woman in black blocked her. "Pay!" She grabbed Lizzy's arm. "Pay, filth, you pay!"

Lizzy tried to pull away, but the woman held her tighter. "Let me go!" Lizzy's arm was pulled up behind her now. "Will!" she shouted, hoping he was still close enough to hear. "Will! Come back!"

Two men pulled the juggler out of the water. They wrinkled their noses at the stink they lifted up with him. He leaped forward, shouting, shaking his fists at Lizzy. The crowd moved back to watch, grinning. The woman let her go, but the juggler picked Lizzy up by the shoulders and lifted her so high, his nose touched hers. He was screaming at her in a language she didn't know, but she understood him. He wanted to kill her, but short of that, he'd take all the money in her purse.

"Let me go!" She tried to push him away, but he held fast, shaking her, water spraying from the bells of his fool's cap.

A group of ruffians, eager for action, whistled and stamped their feet. Lizzy kicked and tried to wriggle free.

"Put her down," a boy's voice called. "It was that dog that made him fall. I saw it all from the bridge. You saw, too, didn't you?" he asked as he moved through the crowd. "She didn't do anything."

Will. It was Will. He'd come back.

The juggler's woman held out her hand. "You pay," she told him, "we let her go." Will shook his head at Lizzy, who'd just kicked her captor in the knee. Reaching into the bag at his waist, he took out two coins, money he'd been saving for his journey, and gave them to the woman in black.

"That's all the plates cost, surely," he said.

"Pah!" The juggler spat, furious, and held Lizzy away from him, dangling her over the murky water.

"Pay *more*," the woman shouted.

"Pitch her in!" yelled someone in the crowd. "Set her down," another called, tossing a coin at the juggler's feet.

"I paid you enough. Let her go," Will insisted.

"Pray you, sir, put me down," Lizzy begged, hoping politeness might work better than a kick in the knee.

"Oh, do," said a man—in English. "This is just too

tedious. I need to talk to that odious child." He pressed a handsome coin into the woman's hand. "And I don't want to do it if she stinks of canal slops."

The woman bit the coin to see if it was real, then raised her eyebrows and nodded to the juggler.

With a shrug, he dropped Lizzy at the edge of the canal. She couldn't get her footing, and she was about to splash in, when Will caught her around the waist and pulled her back again. The juggler smiled, bowed to his audience, and knelt on the puddled stones to scoop up his money.

"Will, you came back!" She grabbed his hand. "I knew you would." It had seemed that all was lost for certain, but now he was here. "You saved me a dunking. You'll stay now, won't you?" The boys were shouting at him from the bridge. "Let the others go."

Behind her, a man cleared his throat loudly. "I believe you mistake, little miss. It was *I* who saved you from the cesspool."

Lizzy turned, giving a quick curtsy to the man who'd paid her ransom. "Oh, thank you, too, good sir," she said. Then she looked at his face and caught her breath. It was the spy! It was the one who'd been dressed in red, only now he wore a doublet of blue brocade, with ivory lace ruffs at his throat and wrists, and a gold ring in his ear. He was Satan, surely, sent by the king.

She would have run, but Will was there—and she had

to talk to him, tell him she did understand, but beg him, still, not to go off to die at sea. "Thank you very kindly," she said to the spy, and turned away.

"I would have sunk like a stone," she told Will, trying to pull him aside. "I followed to beg you to stay." She couldn't give him reasons. All she could do was plead. "Don't go to Amsterdam."

From the bridge, John shouted out in English, "They're after us! They're getting closer. Run, Will! Run!"

Will's back stiffened. "I trusted you."

"It's not true," Lizzy cried. "I told them nothing."

"I sense this brave young man is English, as well," the spy said, clamping his hand on Will's shoulder. "And trying to escape something? My, my. Tell me, do *you* know the whereabouts of William Brewster?"

Will started at the name. He looked at the spy in alarm, then at Lizzy. What did he think? She'd told him that morning of the spies, but he hadn't been listening. "Please. You belong here," she said, but he pulled himself free, bolted, and was gone.

"Run!" called the boys from the bridge. "Run!"

Lizzy tried to run, too, but the spy held her firmly. "Now, Little Miss Lying Is a Sin," said he, "I think the time has come for you to tell the truth."

"I must go, sir," Lizzy said.

"It is the holy Sabbath day," the spy went on. "Why, I

ask myself, is this pious English girl at the fair? Why, I ask, is she not at her Meeting, listening to one of those endless sermons her lawbreaking ministers are so famous for?"

Lizzy looked around for help. Will had gone. He'd left her, believing she had gone back on her promise. And most of the crowd was wandering off, the show over. But the spy kept Lizzy from moving, tightly twisting her wrist. "We can't get anyone in this disgusting town to tell us where that Meeting is," he went on. "Do you know? Are you really one of them? Or are you just an English stray who stole our good Dutch money? I'd like some answers."

Lizzy took a breath and clamped her mouth shut.

"None?" The spy smiled an oily smile. "I've plenty of time. Let us start with this, then, shall we? Who is that courageous lad who ran like a scared rabbit? And why is he off to Amsterdam?"

"That would be William Farley, sir, and I need, please, to go to him," Lizzy told the spy, but he held her fast. "He came with us from Scrooby, he and his mum and pa and brother, John. His father was a—"

"I don't care what his father was. I asked why he was going to Amsterdam." Lizzy considered what to do. She wanted to stick her foot behind his leg, trip him up, and dump him into the canal; but they were too far away for that to work.

"He is off to Amsterdam, kind sir, to—"

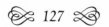

"I am not a kind sir. Remember that. Keep going."

"He was off to Amsterdam to—"

"Tell me a lie and you'll fry in eternal flames, and sooner, I promise you, rather than later."

There was nowhere to go, nothing to do. The boys were gone from the bridge. It was almost time, surely, for afternoon Meeting to begin at the Green Close. And all of the Separatists were there—all except her and Will and John. William Brewster was there.

"He was going, sir . . . to join the . . . to join William Brewster, who, I told you, broke away from us and went to Amsterdam. I didn't want him to go. He is my friend. So, if you'll kindly let me loose . . ."

"I believe I explained that I am *not* kindly. I think you are lying. At the stroke of two, which cometh apace, I am meeting my friend at that perfectly dreadful inn, The Sandwich Arms. We are on our way by hired coach this very afternoon to Amsterdam. But first, little miss, you are going to take me to the Meeting place in Leiden. There are people I would like to question."

"Rat poison, ladies and gents, get your rat poison here. Deadly little cakes, milady." Lizzy could hear the rat catcher hawking his wares. "See for yourselves what my sweet poison pastries can do. Just count the tails of my pretty ones."

"We sail for England on Wednesday next," the spy went

on, leaning down, his foul breath in Lizzy's face. "And we cannot return without firm word, at least, of William Brew— *Aieeeeeeeee!*" he shouted. Dropping Lizzy's wrist, he shook his shoulders violently. Caught in the rolls of the ruff at his neck was a long-tailed, fat, and reeking rat, long dead of arsenic poison, its skin split open from rot.

Lizzy recoiled and ducked. Had the rat catcher spun round so fast that one of his rats flew free? The spy wildly shook it loose. It landed on the toe of his soft leather shoe and he kicked it into the canal. Bits and pieces of it still clung to his collar. As the spy leaned over the canal to vomit, Lizzy broke loose.

Running through the crowded street, she darted past the tightrope walker and up the arch of the bridge, passing, as she did, the other spy. He was staring, mouth agape, at a small brown dancing bear, while a pickpurse lifted his money.

Glancing behind her all the way, ducking into doorways and peeking back, making sure she wasn't followed, Lizzy hurried to the Green Close. It was safety. She could think of nowhere else to go. Meeting was well under way when she slipped back into her place. When it was over, she knew, they would ask her why she had gone and what she had done.

She lowered her eyes. She had done evil. She had gone for Will not because she thought he was wrong to go, but because she was afraid for his life, and, truth to tell, because she wanted him near. All she could do now would be to tell them, as Will had asked, that the boys had left the stink of their work and gone to sea. And God's will be done.

Chapter Seventeen

*W*HEN SHE PASSED BY the windmills at dawn, Lizzy was glad the boy wasn't waiting. She was in no mood for his pranks. Her heart was heavy. Goodman Farley and his wife had clung to each other when she had told them where their sons, John and Will, had gone and why.

"They are good lads," Will's pa had said, giving his wife's hand a squeeze. "Amen," she'd said softly. But they mourned.

"I'll come to help you when I can," Lizzy had promised them. "I told Will I would."

Lizzy sighed as she set to work in the miller's kitchen. Her eyes and nose were running from the chopped onions, but that wasn't all that made them damp. They'd scarcely dried since, after Meeting the night before, she'd told Master Brewster about Will and John. It had stunned him. She didn't admit she'd gone all the way to the fair to try to catch them, and he hadn't asked. He'd been shocked enough that she hadn't told on them. Afterward, he'd met with Will's father and the elders, but she had not heard more.

Lizzy wiped her nose on her sleeve. Cook had sent word that she'd be staying with her daughter for a day or two until she mended, so Lizzy was in charge of the miller's kitchen.

The boy came in from the yard grinning, and she tried to smile back.

"I didn't think I'd see you at the fair, but I did. You were with the spy," he said. "You didn't see me." He leaned toward her and laughed.

Barely listening, Lizzy turned away. She did not want to play games.

"You saw my rat, though," the boy went on. "Did you smell it? It was really stinky."

He circled in front of her, so she had to see his face. "Lizzy, do you hear?" He could hardly wait to tell her. "It was *me*! I was the one who snuck it from the rat catcher. He didn't care. He had lots of them. It was me who wound up and threw it by the tail at that stupid spy. Landed right splat on his fancy collar, too, and on his neck. It was so funny. I got away fast, so nobody caught me, either. Did I save your life?"

Lizzy's mouth fell open, and she shook her head. "You are a scamp. I should have known. My head's been full of worries since then, but still, I've wondered about that rat. Rats almost never just fly through the air like that. Especially being dead."

"And before," he went on, giggling, "before that. You didn't see me before that, either, did you? When you knocked the juggler into the canal? Everybody was laughing so hard at the look on his face. And then at those big eyes you made when he picked you up and shook you. It was so funny. I got it down on paper."

"Down on paper? You mean making those chalk doodles?" Lizzy asked. "And why aren't you off to school? It's well past time."

"I told Madam my mother I had a stomachache from the food at the fair," said the boy. "I ate a whole school of pickled herring and six apple tarts."

Lizzy shook her head. Still, she was, somehow, glad the boy was there. He was a relief. She didn't want to think any more about the day before, how, with Will gone, everything had changed.

"That is why," the boy went on, "Madam my mother let me stay home today. She gave me sweet licorice juice to make me well. I like licorice juice, so I didn't care."

Lizzy picked up the last onion from the basket and peeled off its paper skin. Then she sliced the knife through it four times and began to chop small pieces into a big wooden bowl. "Why do you waste all that good paper? I bet you can't draw any better than I can. I can do good pigs and cats," she added.

The boy smiled broadly as he sat down on the three-legged stool. He took out a fresh piece of paper and a stick of red chalk. "You're good with that knife, too," he told her. "Who taught you?"

"Well, that'd be Sally. Here in town, she took me to work with her when she cooked for a Scotsman. He was a merchant and very rich. Sally's papa was a Scotsman, too. And this merchant, he thought her fine because she made haggis for him. I'll never make it for you."

The boy drew as she talked.

"You have to be born a Scotsman to like it. It's the cut-up lungs and heart and liver of a sheep that you mix with suet and onions and meal, and then you boil it in that same sheep's stomach."

"Can't you stand still?" he asked impatiently.

"Only spoiled little boys can stand still. Why don't you go outside and play knucklebones." When he didn't move, she went on. "I'm busy making chicken *hutspot* for your supper. Sally taught me a good hutspot with onions, carrots, and turnips. She taught me how to pickle fat herring, too. But I'm finest at pancakes. If Cook's lame long enough, I'll show you."

The black cat jumped on the table, purred, and rubbed her elbow, but she shooed it away.

"Up to your old witch tricks," the boy said, laughing. "That cat thinks she lives here now. I think you fed her; that's what I think. I've named her Lizzy. Here, Lizzy kitty."

"Little boy," she told him, drying her hands on her apron, "you stop following me around for a while. I've got something I need to do."

In the yard by the kitchen, a miller was already sitting on the hole in the outhouse. He sent her away, but she was in a hurry, so she squatted on the ground beside the chicken coop. Lifting her skirts and apron high, she made water. Then she stayed there for a moment, her head bowed.

Chattering with the boy kept her problems at bay, but she was going to have to think what to do, now that Will was gone. If she were alone, she could make plans. When she started back to the kitchen, though, the boy was standing in the doorway. She had to give him something to keep him busy.

"All right," she told him. "Since you're not in school today, I'll teach you a thing or two. I'll show you how to draw a proper pig." She picked up a stick and found a patch of dirt against the wall of the house. "Now watch carefully," she told him. "First, I make a shape like a big fat sausage, because that's what a pig is." And she drew it. "Then I make two pointy ears, a squiggly tail—round and round, that's easy—and then a snout." She poked two holes into the snout and scratched down four straight legs.

"There." She handed him the stick. "Now, you try. I've things to do." She rubbed her forehead. "And things to decide. Please, little boy, play by yourself."

Instead of scratching with the stick, he ran inside, and before she could follow, he'd brought out a stack of papers. "Poor Lizzy, you're not smiling much today. These will please you. My pictures always make Madam my mother smile.

"Don't look at the backs. They're just ruined sheets from the printers'," he said. "They give them to me free." He shuffled through the papers, brought one out, and showed it to her, glowing with pride.

Lizzy took the paper, sat on the ground, and stared. The chalk was smudged, but it was a real picture, the kind you could hang on your wall with a frame around it. The drawing was of a juggler, angry, in a fool's cap with bells. His was a real face, too, not just a circle with two dots for eyes and a curved-up mouth. And in his arms, he held a girl.

"Who did this?" she demanded. "Not you, I know that, so don't lie."

He handed her another, waiting for her praise. It was a drawing, like the other, in red chalk, but this one was of a girl peeling an onion, her mess of hair almost hiding her loose white cap. Lizzy hadn't seen herself much, except those times when she'd stared into the wavy water of a canal. But when she put her hand up to her hair and felt her cap askew, she knew this was a picture of her. So, too, was the one with the juggler. It had to be.

"Do you like it?" the boy asked her. "I didn't get the hands right. Hands are very hard to do."

Who'd drawn them? It *had* to be the boy. Nobody else had been in the room just now. No one could have been hiding. But how could he? He was just Fear's age. Maybe *he* was the one who was a witch. How else could he take just a stick of chalk and draw the juggler holding her like that—so real?

"You want to see another?" he asked. "Here's you out by the wall, telling me your Scrooby story."

The picture was clearly Lizzy, her hands out, her mouth open.

Why, this is me, she thought, telling about when I jumped in the moat.

She reached out for the rest of the papers. He tried to hold them back, then let go when one of the sheets began to tear. When she looked at it, she gasped and covered her mouth with her hand. Tears stung her eyes.

"It's me again. Jumping from the windmill. How did you do it? You caught me in the air. My skirt's blowing out and my cap's fallen all the way off. Oh, you are a wicked boy, a *wicked* boy."

"That's stupid! All I did was draw a picture," he said, and tried to grab them back.

"And *this!*" Her head reeled. It was just a sketch, but you could see it was someone squatting by the chicken coop. It could have been anybody from the back, her bottom showing, but it wasn't. She knew it was her.

He shrugged. "Everybody pees," he said. "What's wrong with that?"

"What do you do with these?" Lizzy asked, holding them like a fan in her hand.

"I *draw* them. That's what I do. They're good, aren't they! Here's a splendid one of Cook with her mouth all crooked. And I have one that's good enough to sell. Look, it's of the rat catcher. That was before I stole one of his rats."

"Little boy, you've got to throw the ones of me away," Lizzy said sternly, but she couldn't help staring at her face on the paper. That's what I look like, she thought.

"Throw them away? You're daft. You give those back."

Lizzy held them closer.

"If you don't give them back, I'll . . . I'll spill your hutspot into the fire. I'll . . ." The boy grabbed the sketches from her hand. "You aren't fun anymore. I used to like you, Lizzy Tinker, but now I'm not so sure."

Taking his stack of pictures into the mill yard, he called back, "When you see Madam my mother, tell her I'm feeling much, much better. Tell her I've gone to Old Castle Hill to draw the tops of trees."

Chapter Eighteen

*A*FTER SUPPER THAT NIGHT, at which even Love was silent, Master Brewster led the family in prayer. His text was "Remember now thy Creator in the days of thy youth." At the last amen, Patience tilted her head back and gave Lizzy a knowing smile. They'd been talking about her; Lizzy was sure of it.

She'd prayed for forgiveness, though she hadn't meant to do wrong. She'd prayed to be good. And she'd prayed that Will and John be safe and happy, but maybe that wasn't a proper prayer to make in the Brewsters' house.

"Elizabeth," Master Brewster said sternly, "come here. I want to talk with you. Patience, you put the children in their beds tonight." He unfolded his leather chair next to the door. The top half of the door, usually open to Stink

Alley, was closed, and the air inside was stale. He must, Lizzy thought, be wary of having it open, now that he knows there are spies. He sat down, closed his eyes, and began to puff on a small white clay pipe.

On the long bench, Mary Brewster sat quietly, suckling baby Wrestling.

Lizzy stood in front of him, her heart pounding.

His eyes, when he opened them, were cold and accusing. They were too strong. She looked away. But he wasn't going to scare her, she decided. Will wouldn't want her to fear on his account.

By the light of the lamps, she could see the fine blue lines of grapevines on the crackled tiles that edged the fireplace. Dried fish, sausages, and onions hung from the ceiling above the hearth.

He waited, puffing slowly, until the children had climbed all the way up the circular staircase. Then he said, slowly and evenly, "Elizabeth, this has been a trying day for me."

"Yes, sir," she said, and gave a short curtsy. He looked tired, and sounded it. She'd never felt pity for him before. It had to be hard on him to have the boys leave. Another young man had left just a fortnight ago, without saying why or where. "I'm sorry the boys thought they had to go," she told him. "But Will said they couldn't stomach the work any longer. He said they'd already signed the papers and—"

"Elizabeth!" He cut off her words as sharply and surely as she sliced eel. "Pastor Robinson—indeed, the entire congregation—is shocked that you did not alert us to the Farley boys' foolishness. When our young people stray, we are greatly saddened. But, of course, if they are set on leaving us, there is nothing we can do." He bowed his head. "We do not know God's plan. They are in His hands."

Lizzy bowed her head, too. She was still glad she'd let them go, because she knew they were glad to be gone.

"And the spies, sir?" she asked quickly, looking up. "I hope you've seen the last of them. They were real spies, weren't they? They looked truly wicked, like English spies would, all lace ruffles and bows and fancy gloves." She was so pleased that she'd been able to save Master Brewster. Single-handedly—except for the boy, of course—she'd set the spies on the wrong track. She knew he must be grateful to her for that. "I hope I did the right—"

"Elizabeth," he said with a heavy sigh, "it will do you well to *listen*. Your swelling pride is troublesome. Yes, we've been told that the Englishmen making inquiries have indeed left for Amsterdam." Still, he glanced toward the door. As though talking to himself, he went on. "I did not know the English had discovered that it was I who had written—" He broke off what he was saying and frowned at Lizzy. She stepped back.

"It is not they whom I wish to talk about, Elizabeth. It is *you*."

"Me, sir?"

"Today," he began, "I had business at the printer across from the Eel Market. It is called In the Printery. They have done good work for me in the past, but now I will not use them again. When I arrived, a young boy was there. Do you know what boy I am speaking of?" He leaned forward and skewered her with his cold blue eyes.

She couldn't wriggle free. "Maybe, sir."

"I am going to remind you, Elizabeth, of a passage from Genesis, chapter three, verse seven. It tells what happened because Adam and Eve ate of the forbidden fruit. I want you, Elizabeth, to tell me what it means." He kept his voice quiet and slow, and Lizzy listened. She'd heard the words many times before. "'Then the eyes of them both were opened,'" he quoted, "'and they knew that they were naked, and they sewed fig tree leaves together and made themselves breeches.'"

It was men, not girls, who talked about what the Bible meant. Though Pastor Robinson told them they should all, even the humblest of them, think about it. He believed that anyone who read the Bible—or heard it, if they couldn't read—might see part of the truth that others had missed. Girls and women should think, but they were expected to keep silence. Lizzy pressed her lips together tightly.

Master Brewster leaned toward her, waiting. He'd made her memorize "When pride cometh, then cometh shame." And the verse went on, she remembered, "but with the lowly there is wisdom."

I am lowly enough, she thought. And wise enough, at least, to know what that passage about Adam and Eve means. It means that the boy had showed pictures of her jumping from the windmill with her arms wide and her skirts free, and of her peeing by the chicken coop, her bottom showing, and, worse, of the juggler fighting with her at the fair on the Sabbath. She raised her chin.

"Elizabeth," he asked sharply, "what do those holy words mean to you?"

Baby Wrestling began to cry, a shriek so sharp and long, it made his tiny back arch.

"Oh, Master Brewster, sir," she said in a rush, "the words mean, sir, that we must cover ourselves modest like because the first couple sinned."

"That is close enough," he told her. "And the pictures the boy showed those men? Were you modestly covered in those? It *was* you, wasn't it!" He was losing the reins on his voice.

"He's just a little boy, sir, but he draws very well for his age, and he's just drawing everything he sees all the time, and—"

"*Did* you jump from the windmill with your skirts above your knees? And are you *ashamed?*"

"I caught hold of the mill wing because I thought he was in need. He's just a lad, sir. He was playing."

"The printers laughed at his drawings," Master Brewster told her. "And what they were laughing at was *you*. Flying through the air. Squatting, skirts at your waist. And being embraced, brazenly, by a juggler at the fair. You went to the fair on the Sabbath! On the *Sabbath*! It was you. The boy wouldn't say your name, but I knew."

His face was red with anger. His pipe had gone out, and he shifted it from one hand to the other. "Are you, then, not ashamed?" he shouted as Wrestling continued to shriek and wail. "Do you refuse to be ashamed?"

"I . . . I . . . I didn't know he was drawing me at the time, sir. I only—"

"Did you jump from the windmill?"

"Yes sir, I—"

"And did you go to the fair on God's holy day and while there lewdly embrace a juggler?"

"I did not, sir. I did not. A dog ran against the juggler when I was chasing after Will. And he fell in the canal and two of his plates broke. You can see from his face, sir,

❧ *145* ❧

he wasn't hugging me. He was shaking me because I'd—"

The clay pipe slid from Master Brewster's hand and shattered on the tile floor. Wrestling screamed.

"Just walk the baby, Mary," he said sharply. "Do *something* to keep him quiet."

He lowered his head and rubbed his temples. "A juggler in his fool's cap was holding you on the Lord's Day. And yet you are not ashamed."

Sitting straight and tall again, he said, "Step closer, Elizabeth, and listen carefully. You may no longer work in the miller's kitchen. It is not wholesome. The young boy of the house and his disgusting drawings are an offense to us. Further, you may not work in any place that requires you to live with a Dutch family." His hands were shaking. "We no longer trust you."

He's often said that anger turns a man into a monster, Lizzy thought. He must hate it that I've made him so angry.

He lowered his voice and went on gravely. "Your father did not break your willfulness when you were a child. That he did not was a fault in him. Still, he would have been stung by what you have done. You did not honor him. You do not honor me. You poison my house. It is a true blessing that Jehovah in His great mercy took your father before he could hear of this disgrace."

Lizzy's face turned red. He should not fault her papa so.

He leaned toward her. "And our Love, at his tender age, has begun, since your arrival, to sing taunting songs to his sister Fear. We believe it is you who pollute his young soul."

"But, sir, I—" She would not have him believe it.

"Tomorrow morning, Elizabeth, you will go to the miller's house. You will remain only long enough to say that your work there is at an end."

"Yes sir." Lizzy bowed her head and knelt to pick up the broken pipe. It was hard for her to breathe. It is *not* a mercy that Papa is gone, she thought. He would have listened to me. Sally would have listened to me. They would have known I did no harm to Love's soul.

"They need women to fold cloth at the fulling mill. You are strong enough. That should keep you busy and out of harm's way," Master Brewster said firmly. He stood and turned away from her.

The baby stopped crying and began to coo gently.

He meant for her to go now. He did not want to hear her say anything more. "Good night, Master Brewster," she said to the back of his head. "Good night, Mistress Brewster," she said, pausing. "Thank you for taking me in when Papa died."

Starting up the circular steps toward bed, she breathed as evenly as she could. She knew she had to leave. I can't stay with the Brewsters, she thought desperately. I can't ever be right enough here. If I were a boy, she thought, I'd follow Will tomorrow and go to sea. There is no way, though, being a girl, that I can run so far. But somehow, soon, I'll go.

She turned again to the silent room. "Good night, baby Wrestling," she said. "Sleep well."

Chapter Nineteen

LIZZY PICKED UP HER SHOES and began to tiptoe to
the stairs. The morning had come too soon. There
had been no cries in the dark, no Satan alarms from Fear,
but no answers, either, to the questions she'd asked
throughout the night. Where shall I go? When? How?

Lizzy yelped. She'd stepped on something in the dark.
Love's marble. She could tell by the feel of it. It shot off
the ball of her foot and hit the chamber pot with a *ping*.

Breathing lightly, she held herself still. She didn't want
to wake them.

"Lizzy?" Love called, sleep in his voice. She didn't
answer. "I know it's you," he said. "Where you going?" She
could sense him slipping out of bed. That wouldn't do.

"Shhhhhh," she said, bending over him. "I'm going to

work. You go back to sleep." She pulled the cover up to his chin. "Close your eyes and dream about marbles. I just stepped on the one you lost, the new one Will gave you. It's here somewhere."

He was quiet till she started down the circular steps.

"Lizzy!" She stopped. "Are you going to that nasty place? Patience says you can't work there anymore. She says Father said you snuck off to go to the fair. She says you're a bad girl."

Lizzy closed her eyes. How could they keep her with them if they thought so ill of her?

"Go back to sleep. Please, Love," she whispered. "Later, you find your new marble and then dig a good wide hole outside. I'll bring back a round stone or two and play you a game of Holy Bang. All right?"

He whimpered. "You aren't bad, are you?"

"I'm good at marbles," she told him, "but if you practice all day, it may be that you'll win." She headed cautiously down the steps toward the fireplace.

After poking the coals and laying on a small tower of peat, she looked into the hanging bread basket. There was half a loaf of good wheat bread left, but she couldn't eat. Her stomach was cramped with worry.

Passing out of Stink Alley, Lizzy walked slowly along the old worn stones toward the Gerritzen place. She went over the questions of the night. Master Brewster was an elder. She couldn't disobey his order to leave her job. She would tell Cook. And then what? What was there for her to do except bend her back folding cloth?

She had to tell the boy. In spite of everything, she liked him. He was exactly what Master Brewster didn't like. The boy said "I want." The boy often lied. The boy had been prideful, showing those pictures of her at the printer. And it wasn't just pictures of her he'd shown. There was one of Cook with fire in her eyes and a fine one of the rat catcher. It was true they were very good pictures. He had reason to be proud.

The boy liked her, too, she decided. He'd begged to hear her stories. He'd flung a dead rat to set her free. And he'd even named a cat for her.

Lizzy could hear the windmills creaking well before she saw them. They were spinning fast this morning. The breeze was whipping in, pushing mounds of high dark clouds before it. She stopped and pulled her cap more firmly on her bound-up braids.

It will be a while, she thought, before the work bell rings. Still, no matter how early she'd come before, the boy had always been there first. Yet he wasn't waiting on the river wall. She circled the bigger of the two windmills, the one she'd swung on. No boy. Perhaps the fair food really *had* made him sick. But that was two days ago.

"*Ohhhhlizzzzzzzzzeeeeeeeeee!*" The sound swelled up

behind her. Goose bumps prickled her arms and the back of her neck, though this time she knew exactly who it was.

She kept her back turned to him. She had to let him know that showing those drawings had brought her pain.

"Lizzeeeeeeee, are you angry with me?" he asked.

Whirling around, she looked him in the eye and crossed her arms. "Do you think I should be?"

"I wasn't sure," he began, taking giant steps around her. "That Brewster man didn't like my pictures. I didn't know it was him till one of the printers called him by name. I always show my pictures to the printers. They like them. Sometimes they even take them in pay for clean paper. The Brewster man spoke good Dutch. He wanted the pictures, but I wouldn't let him have them. He's not my favorite man. Was he very angry with you?"

"He was angry with me, yes," Lizzy told him. "But, no, I'm not angry with you. I was, but I'm not anymore."

The boy stopped right at her feet, then hopped off his stilts. He was wearing his floppy red velvet cap. "It's windy and it may rain," he said. "Before long, they'll have to pull the canvas back from the wings to slow them down. I can tell that, even though I'm not a miller yet. Do you think I should be a miller, Lizzy?"

She looked him over. "Might be good for you. But I don't think so. You'd be an awful miller. You'd be off drawing pictures of pigs while the barley burnt." She picked up his stilts. "I came early today because I've got something to tell you. Can I walk on these?"

He held them steady for her, and she stepped up. "How do you hold your arms?" she asked him. She walked on the stilts for two full steps, then fell off. He helped her back up and she began to take big strides, walking around in circles.

"I have something to tell you, too," he said, following her. "It's not a good something, either. Cook told Madam my mother that you're lazy. What she means is, she doesn't want anybody in her kitchen better than she is. That's what I think. Cook is mad at me, too. She found the stack of pictures. The one on top was the one of her making that frog face in the wheelbarrow, so she just threw them all in the fire."

Lizzy lowered her head, walked on the stilts once around the boy, then hopped off. "It was very bad of you to draw me squatting out by the chicken coop. That made me mad, and I mean it."

The boy nodded. "It wasn't my best one. Your head was too big."

"I liked the one of me jumping," she said. "I never told you that, but I liked it. It was sneaky of you to draw it, and that's the truth. But you made it look like I went up really high, higher than I'd ever go."

"Sir my father doesn't like me drawing pictures," he said. "Madam my mother, she likes them a lot if they're holy ones from Bible stories, but I don't do many of those. What I was going to tell you is that Madam my mother liked your hare and your hutspot, but—"

"She doesn't want me here anymore, does she?" said Lizzy.

He shook his head. "And there's nothing I can do. I tried. Cook'll give you money for a week's work, though," he said. "I told Madam my mother that was only fair. Cook's daughter carted her back here last night, well after you were gone. Said she missed her bed here. She complained you'd left her kitchen a mess, but you didn't. What was it you were going to tell me?"

She started to explain, then thought for a moment and shrugged it off. "Nothing," she told him, and wandered over toward the big windmill. Canvas covered only half of each arm's wooden framework, and the wind had died down, so the arms spun slow and even. The miller wouldn't need to pull the canvas back more after all to keep them from spinning too briskly.

"I never rode the wing all the way round like I told you I did," the boy said. "I lied."

"Little boy," she said, "you must not do that. You know very well that every lie scars your soul."

She reached out and touched the wooden frame as it

swept by. "What do you suppose you could see from the top?" she asked, cupping her hands around her eyes and looking up. "It's higher up there than I've ever been. It's higher even than Old Castle Hill. I'm sure it's as high as a mountain. I wonder. If you rode to the top, could you see all the way to Amsterdam?"

"If it was clear, maybe," said the boy. "Not today. If it was clear, I bet you could see to the Indies. Or the Garden of Eden."

"There's a hole in the clouds," Lizzy told him, pointing, "over there. See? Should I go up and take a look?"

As she watched the wheel turn, questions whirled in her head. What would happen next? To her. Her job was gone. Will was gone. She watched as the windmill wing brushed the clouds. She yearned to ride it. It was too far up. It was too risky. It made no sense at all to do it. But when the next wing reached as high as her nose, Lizzy reached out and grabbed its wooden frame. She'd just swing a bit. The arm slowed. Then, with a sudden gust of wind, it pulled up with a jerk. She gasped.

The boy would grab her feet. Then she'd let go. She waited for the tug, but this time he didn't try to stop her.

As the wing moved higher, she remembered from before the strangeness of rising, of having her arms stretch to different lengths as the mill turned. Then suddenly, she remembered, too, the awful fear that had filled her just before she'd jumped, and she tasted it again.

In the river, two swans, their wings spread wide, were skimming over the water. Lizzy could see them flying. The boy, on the ground, could only hear them flapping. The windmill wing was halfway up. Already her shoulders ached.

"Can you see the Indies yet?" the boy called.

She looked down at him, and a wave of dizziness made her arms tremble. She unclenched her teeth. "No," she called back as strongly as she could, "I see America." She carefully breathed in. And out. "North and South." She smiled. He would like that. Her fingers were numb. Maybe they were slipping. It was hard to tell. If she fell, she would die. She was that far up. "And in the ocean—" she gulped in air—"there's a great golden fish. Spouting water."

Her wing of the mill was now almost straight up. She had reached the top of the mountain. Standing upright, she rested her feet firmly on a wooden cross slat and gaped at the view beneath the dark clouds. In the middle distance was Old Castle Hill and St. Peter's Church, where she'd sat with Will on the square. Joy rose in her throat.

But the arm of the mill started down so quickly. She hugged the slats tightly with her arms and legs. She wanted to stay standing at the top, breathing the air and feeling free. But the arm of the mill kept moving down.

Below her, the boy was waving with both hands.

Her stomach turned. She was glad she hadn't eaten the bread. It would, just then, have come right back up. *Aieeeeeeeeeeee!* rang in her ears, the cry of the watchman as he fell.

Pressing her whole body into the wood, Lizzy buried her head in the canvas and breathed as slowly as her heart would let her. The more the wing swung, the more her head pointed to the ground. She clamped her skirt between her knees.

Now the sky was at her feet. Her mouth was dry and salty. She loosened her fingers from the windmill slats and worked her way around till her legs could hang loose. When she put her feet on land again, things would never be the same. She had flown.

Lamps flickered on in houses far down the canal. Lightning cut through the black clouds. The swans were honking.

When the windmill's arm finally pointed straight to the ground, almost touching it, Lizzy still held on. The boy had to pull her off.

She lay on the hard ground, panting, as the wing started up again.

"Papa," she said, gulping in air, "would have been proud of me for being so strong."

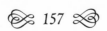

"You did it. You *did* it!" the boy shouted. "I thought I'd have to catch you when you fainted and fell off. All the way round, I held my breath. I couldn't even draw you doing it, I was watching so hard. What was it like up there? Could you really see America?"

"No," she answered quickly, "not even Amsterdam. So don't you go trying it." It'd be just like him to ride a wing all the way around only because she had. She lay there, winded, looking at the darkening sky. "You can't see anything up there but fog. Nothing."

A workman powdered with malt came scurrying around the base of the mill. "What are you scamps up to? Swinging on those wings again? You scat now! Away! I don't want you hanging round this mill. I'll tell your father, young man, and he'll be harsh." He shrugged. "As harsh as he ever gets with you."

Rain began to fall, fat drops of it.

Lizzy crawled a step, then got up on unsteady feet. She flapped the dust from her apron and skirts. Then they both ran to the river wall.

"Oh, little boy," Lizzy said, leaning against the wall, "I am so sorry to leave your house. I'll miss you. I will." Even though, she thought, if it hadn't been for him, Master Brewster wouldn't have lost his temper at me. Still, if it hadn't been for him, I wouldn't have flown so high and felt so free, either.

"I have to go," he told her. "I have to go to school, at least for a little while. I promised Sir my father." He turned and ran toward the bridge.

He was halfway across the yard before she remembered. "I brought a present for you," she called, and reached for the bag at her waist.

"I'll leave early, then. I'll meet you. On Old Castle Hill. As soon as the rain stops."

He ran toward the bridge, then turned back. It was pouring now. "I hope it's not a book in Latin!" he called. "If it is, I don't want it."

Chapter Twenty

T HE RAIN FELT GOOD to Lizzy. It cooled her down. She caught her breath, though, when the Yarn Market's bell rang. It was time for work to begin, but she had no work to begin. As she headed toward the house to collect her wages, she steeled herself against Cook's ranting.

But when Lizzy entered the kitchen, Cook just smirked and waited, sitting on the three-legged stool, a tankard of beer in her hand. In a fireplace kettle, the hutspot was bubbling gently. It was the stew Lizzy had made the day before.

"Good morning, Cook," Lizzy said. "I'm glad to see the poultice worked. Maybe you know already. I'm leaving. I've come for the money I earned."

"You're not *leaving*; you're being tossed out," Cook said. "On my say-so. You want money? For what?"

She's trying to scare me, Lizzy thought. But I don't scare easy now, do I? I rode a windmill wing.

Lizzy looked her square in the eye, took out her sharp knife, and speared a piece of chicken from the hutspot kettle. Flying had made her hungry.

"Friday, I wrung three chickens' necks and peeled, chopped, and scrubbed. Saturday, I cleaned and larded that hare good and quick with my own sharp knife and made a very good supper." She picked out a bite of turnip with it. "Yesterday, I fixed this fine stew."

She held out her hand.

Cook glanced away from Lizzy's eyes, shrugged, and reached into her worn woolen pouch. Lizzy watched carefully as she counted out the coins.

"The boy said I'd get paid for a week."

"The boy lied," Cook said.

The boy hadn't lied. He'd truly thought they'd pay her. Lizzy was sure of it. She wouldn't ask again. She didn't want to get wages, anyway, for more than she'd earned.

"I paid nine duiten for cookies and nobody paid me back," she said instead, her eyes locked on Cook's. "And I think I'll stay right here until somebody does."

The black cat slipped into the room and rubbed Lizzy's leg. Lizzy leaned over, scratched its neck, and grinned.

"Good Lizzy," she told it. The cat purred loudly.

"Scat," Cook hissed. The cat slipped behind Lizzy's skirts. Lizzy speared another turnip and chewed it slowly.

"Here," Cook told her, counting out nine more coins. "And good riddance to bad rubbish."

"Thank you," Lizzy told her. "Good day."

When she stepped into the mill yard, rain whipped her face. The wind was blowing so hard that two millers were out tending the sails. One of those sails was hers now, but already, even looking closely, she couldn't tell which.

Heading through the rain, she walked straight to the bakery. She owed Jan the cookie cloth. It was folded up in the bag at her waist.

The oven doors at the bakery were flung open, and heat was blasting out. Jan was at the ovens, the sleeves of his white shirt rolled up. He was pulling out trays of brown-crusted rolls with a long-handled paddle and sliding them off onto racks. His father, kneading dough, waved a sticky hand at her. "Ho, Liz," he called. "Blow the bread horn up front, will you? Let them know the *broodjes* are ready. From what I hear, you're good at it, and we need a customer or twelve."

Lizzy lifted the sheep horn from its hook, pressed it tight against her lips, and blew three long blasts. They were almost as loud and shrill as the ones she'd scared the spies with. Though Master Brewster had said the men had gone, she glanced about, searching for them. No spies. Not even in the shadows. If Master Brewster made them mad enough with what he wrote about the king, she thought, they'll be back, or others like them. She blew the horn again to scare the thought away.

"There," she called back toward the ovens, "that ought to bring them out." That, she thought, and the smell of such good fresh bread. No smell better.

When Jan joined her at the front of the shop, his face was flushed from the heat of the ovens. He took the horn from her and blew it yet again. "Broodjes, tasty hot broodjes!" he called. But the rain was beating down hard, and no customers came running. His long blond hair, pasted to his head with sweat, almost reached his shoulders. He peeled off his white baker's hat and fanned himself with it.

"You here for more cookies?" he asked when she handed him the wrapping cloth. "Wish we had some, but my mother's unsteady on her feet. She's swelled up big." He blew the horn again. "Hot broodjes! Get 'em while they're hot!" he cried.

The rain rushed in, but no customers. "And my two little brothers keep her winded. It's going hard for her."

Lizzy shook her head. "I pray for her safe delivery."

"Broodjes, then?" he asked her. "None better."

"No," she said, "no cookies or rolls for me." She smiled. "No job, either. The last cook called me a witch for

skinning a hare so fast." She shrugged. "I'm just returning the cloth. Thank you for letting me use it."

A little girl came running in from the rain, a length of soft brown corduroy flung over her shoulder. Jan packed six hot rolls in it.

"I was thinking," Lizzy said when the girl had gone, "with your mother doing poorly, I could come tomorrow and help. I make good pastry. Sally taught me. You wouldn't even need to pay me. I have to get a proper job folding cloth, Master Brewster says, but for now I'd like to help out. I can't make those fancy letter cookies, but—"

Jan held up his hand for her to wait while he rushed back to slide another batch of broodjes out of the oven. She could see Jan and his father talking inside the bakery, their heads leaning together over a mound of rising dough.

The rain began to slow. A woman with a crisp red-and-white-checked cloth in her basket ducked in and asked for a dozen rolls. Lizzy had already packed them up neatly by the time Jan returned to take the woman's money.

"Father says thank you for your offer. He'll try you out, and gladly," Jan told her, smiling. "Unless being a folder is what you really want to do. It'll bow your back, though, you know."

"Oh, Jan," she told him, "of course it isn't. Sally made me a cook."

 *164*

Jan nodded. "Father says if your pies and tarts are half so good as hers were, you'll do fine. He'll give you fair pay. Mother will come in the morning, he says, if she's up to it, to get you started."

Lizzy flushed with happiness. She told herself not to hope. They were just going to let her make some cookies. It might last for only a day. But Jan had talked of pies and tarts. Did he mean . . .

Customers had begun to press into the small shop, so Lizzy couldn't ask. She turned to go.

"Tomorrow," she told Jan, "I'll be here well before the Yarn Market's bell tolls."

The apple crop was huge this year. Maybe she could make sweet apple tarts with her good flaky crusts. And they *were* flaky. That wasn't prideful. That was true.

Lizzy skipped through puddles. Then she stopped and laughed. She hadn't skipped since Scrooby.

Chapter Twenty-one

*T*HE RAIN HAD STOPPED, and the sun shone down through patches of clouds. Steam rose from the cobblestones. Lizzy leaned over the Eel Market bridge and frowned at her reflection in the canal. The Brewsters don't trust that face, she thought, but I do. I would take it to Brazil or the Indies or even Amsterdam, but I can't run afar like Will did. Besides, the misery he ran away from is still clinging to his mum and pa.

She picked up a stone and threw it in the water. Her reflection rippled. I don't even want to leave, she thought. This place is my home. Her thoughts moved on. I wonder if I could help Will's parents, and help me, too? The waves faded, and she watched her face slowly take shape again.

The sky was clear. Could the boy be on Old Castle Hill already? Once he was in school, would they let him out just because he said he wanted to go? They had more control of him at Latin School than at home, surely.

But when she arrived, the boy was there, sitting at the top of the high stone steps, his red velvet cap pulled over his ears.

"Where's my present?" he called down when he saw her.

She hitched up her skirt and ran the steps two at a time. "Little boy," she said when she reached the top, "your manners are dreadful. You shouldn't ask about presents first. First you should say, 'Hello, Lizzy. How are you? Have you found other work?' And I would say, 'I'm fine, little boy. It's nice of you to ask. In fact, I *have* found a new job, at Blaeus' bakery. What do you think of that?'"

It wasn't *quite* true. Jan had just said they'd try her out, but it felt good to say.

Inside the tower on Old Castle Hill, the round field of trees and grass was way too wet to play in. The boy clambered up the steps that led to a lookout walkway near the top. When he got there, he called down, "I think that's good, but what's my present?"

She sighed, shook her head, and followed him up the flight to the highest ledge. There they leaned out the wide notches at the top of the wall, where soldiers had once stood with guns aimed at invaders. Or with buckets of hot oil. Or with spears, in the old, old days. A shaggy white dog on the hill below them looked up and barked.

"You can see Sir my father's two mills, just there." The boy pointed. "That's where you rode the wing all the way round. I wish I could, but I think I won't ever be that brave." He peered at her bag. "Is it something to eat, my present? I'm getting hungry. Did you smash it when you fell off the windmill?"

"I didn't fall off. You pulled me off. And, no," she told him, "it didn't break. I looked."

They settled their elbows on the wall and watched the clouds skid briskly away.

"Remember when I told you about how we tried to leave England?" she asked him.

"They threw the men in prison and sent the women and children home," he said. "I remember. Yes, that's good. Tell me the rest of the story."

"Well," she began, "once the men got out of prison, it took us half a year more before we finally escaped and got to Amsterdam. At least some of us did." And she told him how she'd boarded the Dutch merchant ship with the men and boys and how the boat full of women and children got stuck in the mud.

"This sounds like a story from a book. You're not making it up, are you?" he asked her.

"I'm not," she said. "Lying—"

"I know," he said. "It's a sin." He took off his red velvet cap and draped it on her head. It covered her own cap completely and lapped down a little over one eye. "I've got an idea. I'm going to draw you wearing my cap," he said.

Lizzy shook her head. "Oh no, you're not. You'd just show it to the printers—or to Master Brewster," she told him, taking it off.

"Not this time," he said, putting it back on her. "I promise. Now, hold still."

She reached up to touch it. He must really want to draw me, she thought. He's forgotten all about his present. "Does your cap have lice in it?" she asked him.

He scratched his head. "I expect so."

She lifted it off, inspected the inside, and, finding no bugs, put it back on. From his leather pouch, the boy took a stick of chalk and a sheet of paper. It had only a little printing smudged on the back. He unfolded it and placed it on a smooth brick. Looking at her closely, he began to draw.

"I'll draw," he told her. "You tell me the rest of the story. Only don't move anything but your mouth."

He was always scratching away on paper as if it was something he had to do. She'd stopped paying it much attention. But this time was different. She knew how well he could draw now and she knew he was drawing a picture of her. Reaching up, she touched the hat again. She'd never worn velvet before. It felt rich and elegant. She tilted her chin up.

Lizzy told him how the big Dutch ship had sailed away while soldiers with guns arrested the women and children, who were trapped and weeping on the shore.

The boy leaned close over the paper and made a series of short, swift strokes.

Keeping her head as steady as possible, Lizzy told him about the storm at sea. She told about the creaking ship, how it had heaved and surged in the waves, about the fourteen drenching days and nights when she was sure she'd soon be a skeleton among the fishes. With a start, she thought about Will maybe now already at sea again, and she lowered her head.

"Stop it!" he told her. "Tip your head back up the way it was. You're moving too much." He twirled the tip of the chalk around on a patch of brick to sharpen it. Then he touched the paper with it lightly. "And what did you bring me?"

She reached into her bag. "Here's the spies' bribe money," she told him, handing him the coins, "and welcome to it, but that's not the present."

Shaking his head, he slipped the coins into his leather pouch.

She laughed and held her chin higher. The boy narrowed

his eyes and drew. Finally, he put the chalk down.

"I've just a little way to go," he said.

"So have I, and then I'll give you the present." She lost her pose and leaned toward him. "I'm giving it to you because you helped save Master Brewster. And because you saved me, you truly did, with that dead rat. And because I flew on your windmill. It's a big present. Big to me. A sailor aboard that ship gave it to me. He said it brought good luck. And if you're going to make your way drawing pictures, you'll need good luck."

The boy sat up tall and tucked the chalk over his ear. "Good luck? Me? I won't need good luck," he told her. "Do tell me what it is. I *want* it!"

She hesitated a moment, then reached into the bag at her waist. "Close your eyes and hold out your hand." Watching to see that his eyes stayed shut, she wrapped her fingers around the white-speckled cowrie shell the old sailor had given her six years before. Last night, before she'd gone to bed, she'd untied the ribbon on her doll, Hannah, and taken it out. She'd always thought of the shell as Hannah's heart. Six years it had stayed there, a hidden treasure. It felt cool now in her palm. She ran her thumb across its rough bottom ridges, where the cowrie once had slid across the floor of the sea. It was a rare thing. She put it in his open hand.

He clamped it tightly in his fist.

What if he doesn't care about the shell? Lizzy thought suddenly. What if he just tosses it over the wall at the dog? She almost reached to grab it back.

The boy opened his eyes, uncurled his fingers, and stared. Then he began to jump up and down. "I *love* seashells!" he cried, throwing his arms around her. "And this is the best one ever." He held it up to the sun. "Ever. I love it, Lizzy. Thank you!"

He'd thanked her. The boy without manners had thanked her.

She felt she hardly knew him. He was acting like an eight-year-old boy. He drew so well and talked so smart, she'd almost forgotten.

"I won't just sketch it," he said, "I'll do an engraving of it. The printers are showing me how. It's hard to do, but I'm learning. Lizzy, this is so fine." He turned the shell over and over, looking closely at every curve. Then he tucked it into his leather bag. "And all I've got for you is your picture. I drew it especially to give you." He took the stick of chalk from behind his ear and touched the page with it lightly. "If Cook hadn't burnt the others, I'd have let you have the one with you jumping."

He held the new picture out so she could see.

It was her all right. And she wasn't doing anything she shouldn't do in it. He hadn't made her tidy, though—just drawn her head the way it was. No lies in his pictures, anyway. With only a little stick of black, he'd put her down on paper, his cap cocked over one of her eyes, clumps of curly black hair sticking out from under it. What could she say?

"You're very good," she told him. "Maybe you won't need a *lot* of luck, just one small cowrie shell full." Looking at the picture closely, she said, "I've got my mouth open."

"You always do."

"The cap really looks velvet. How did you do that? And you made my hair all curly with rain. Do I have dirt on my chin like that?"

"It's a scrape," he said, "from falling off the mill." He paused. "Do you like it?"

She stared long at the picture. "It's wonderful," she told him finally. "Thank you." She wished she could still jump up and down with joy, the way he had. "Wonderful and then again wonderful." Looking at it again, she said, "It looks finished to me. You told me you had a little way to go."

"I need to sign my name," he said, "so you'll remember who drew it."

He'd left a space at the bottom. On it, across the whole page, he wrote in tall letters, "Rembrandt Harmensz van Rijn, 1614."

She looked at the letters and blinked. "That's a long

name," she told him. "How do you say it? I can't read."

"Maybe sometime I'll teach you how. It's a good thing to know if you don't have to go to school to learn it." He pronounced it for her. "*Rembrandt*, that's how you say it. The boys at school chant it over and over and laugh."

"It's a little old-fashioned maybe, but it's a nice name," Lizzy told him. "Rembrandt," she repeated it. "Truly. I like it."

"Takes up too much room on the paper," he said. "Should I just use initials next time? *R* for the Rembrandt part. *H* for Harmensz, son of Harmen." He pointed to the word. "And then for van Rijn, because I live on the Rhine River, I could just write *vR*. What do you think?"

"Good." Lizzy nodded. "When you sign your whole name, it's almost as big as the picture. Still, I'm glad you signed it full. When you get to be the most famous maker of pictures in the whole world, I'll point to your name, your name right there, and show people." She laughed. He didn't.

"Artist," he said. "Most famous *artist* in the whole world. My father is going to enroll me at the university. He thinks I'm going to be a lawyer, but I'm not. An artist is what I'm going to be."

Lizzy took his red cap off her head and handed it to him. "I'll roll my picture up tight and hide it inside Hannah," she said, packing it away in her bag. It would, she thought, take the place of the shell as Hannah's new heart.

"Race you to the bottom!" He ran toward the steps of the tower.

Once outside, he skidded down the wet grass to the bottom of the hill. She took the steps. He won. "I have to go back to school," he told her. "If I'm gone too long, they send for Sir my father. Are you off to the bakery? It's a good place. I'll come when I have money and buy your pretzels and pancakes."

"I'm not going there now. I don't start until tomorrow, but I'll be there the next day and the next. They'll keep me on." She grinned at him. "Last job, they didn't."

He tucked his head down. "I'm sorry," he told her. "It was my fault Cook fired you."

"No, it's not. Besides, she would never even have hired me without you. Right now, though, I've got things to do. My friend Will Farley, you never met him—"

"The one who called you Missy Puke Stockings?"

"That was his brother, John. Will calls—called—me Lizzy-bit." She took a deep breath. "Well, Will and his brother both ran off to sea on Sunday. That's why I was at the fair, trying to stop them. I've just decided that what I'm going to do is talk to their mum and pa today. I'm going to ask them if I can live at their house now. It's a spare place, but with the boys gone, they'll be lonely and needing help."

"I hope it's not in Stink Alley," the boy said. "I hate that name."

She shook her head. "It's in the new part of town. Stink Alley is where I'm going first, though."

"When I do a fine engraving of my shell, I'll think about you," Rembrandt said. He took it out of his leather bag and rubbed it between his palms. "I'll think about you on that boat. Oh," he said, remembering, "those women and children stuck in the mud. You didn't tell me. Did they all die in the end?"

The boy's school was only two blocks away from Stink Alley, so Lizzy walked along with him. Rembrandt kicked a loose stone along the cobbles.

"Here's what happened," she began. "The soldiers came roaring up, all ready to shoot to kill, and all they got was a boatful of women and babies howling mad that their ship had sailed without them. Sally said the soldiers were really disappointed," Lizzy told him. "They didn't know what to do. They took them in all muddy to a constable. He didn't know what to do with them, either, Sally said. The constable decided they weren't guilty of anything except obeying their husbands, who'd already escaped across the sea."

"Herring, sweet pickled herring," a vendor called. "Makes your mouth water. Get your sweet pickled herring."

"You want a pickled herring?" the boy asked. "I've got a lot of money." They stopped and looked into the bucketful of them. The vendor knew the boy and gave them two sweet fat ones.

Lizzy was hungry. Still, she chewed her fish slowly, letting its juices trickle down her throat. Then after she wiped her hands and mouth on her apron, she finished her story as they walked. "Well, that first constable just threw up his hands. He sent the women and their babies to another constable. And he didn't know what to do, either. Nobody'd arrest them. After all, they were just women. Anyway, sooner or later, in batches, everybody got to Holland. Sally was among the last of them. She'd hung back, cooking in a tavern to make a little money to put in our pockets."

Lizzy reached down and picked up the stone the boy had been kicking. It was almost round. "There's a game called Holy Bang," she told him. "You know it?"

The boy shook his head. "Must be English."

"You dig a wide hole. Somebody puts a knicker in it. Then somebody else shoots another knicker at it. If your knicker hits the knicker in the hole three times in a row, you get to keep it.

"I'm going to win at Holy Bang. And the little boy I win

from—his name is Love—I'll get him to promise me never ever again to tell his sister Fear that Satan will get her in the dead of night. He'll promise me so he can get his marble back. And I'll make him tell me what lying is."

"A sin," said Rembrandt solemnly.

"A sin it is. I'll give him back his knicker and tell him to take good care of it because it was Will's."

"That's a bribe," the boy told her.

"Ah, yes," she said, "I suppose it is. It may even work."

They walked awhile in silence while Lizzy thought of her plan.

"Master Brewster won't be home yet, since today is a day he goes to a student's lodgings to tutor," she said, as much to herself as to the boy. "So then I'll go straightaway to the house where Will used to live. His father will still be working, but I'll tell his mother that before he left, Will asked me to look after them. I'll ask if I can stay there. They have known me since Scrooby, all my life. They love me. They loved my mother and my papa, and Sally, too, all of them gone. They will let me stay.

"Then I'll go back to the Stink Alley house and pack up my things. For her kindness in feeding me, I'll give Mistress Brewster the few coins I've saved. I'll say, 'Thank you very much,' and then, when Master Brewster comes home, I'll tell them all good-bye."

"He'll be angry," the boy told her. "He was very angry with me."

"Yes. But he'll let me go. He doesn't like having me there. He told me last night that I was poison. He thinks I make his children feel too free." And, she thought with a start, it may just be true.

They'd reached the square at St. Peter's Church. Rembrandt, drawing in the air with his piece of chalk, went slowly off toward school. In his other hand, he held fast to the speckled cowrie shell. Lizzy turned away. Then she tossed the round stone knicker as high as she could and caught it just before it touched the ground.

At Meeting, they'll be cold, she thought, but they'll forgive me. She raised her chin. They know I sent the spies away. They know that if it wasn't for me, William Brewster could be on his way back to England. They know now that he has to be wary, always.

"Lizzy," the boy called to her. He'd run back. "Every time I go to the bakery for pancakes, you know what I'm going to do? I'm going to stand right at the very place where you tricked those spies and I'm going to tell everybody how you did it. And then I'm going to tell them how you rode Sir my father's windmill all the way round and how you almost got thrown in the canal by a mad juggler." He smiled. "And none of it will be a lie."

She grinned at him. "Little boy—Rembrandt—you may be a very good artist, but I think that Cook is right. You are a terrible scamp."

"Little girl—Lizzy—I expect you both are right." He blew his breath on the cowrie shell and rubbed it on his doublet to make it shine. Waving it at Lizzy, he turned again toward school.

Lizzy slipped the stone knicker into her bag, took a long, deep breath, and, smiling, turned down the dark, narrow passage of Stink Alley.

Afterword

THE FIRSTHAND STORY of the Separatists' voyage from Scrooby to Holland to America is told in *Of Plymouth Plantation 1620–1647*, a memoir written by William Bradford, the second governor of the Plymouth Colony. In it, he wrote about one of the reasons the Separatists decided to leave Leiden:

> *For many of their children that were of best dispositions and gracious inclinations, having learned to bear the yoke in their youth and willing to bear part of their parents' burden, were oftentimes so oppressed with their heavy labours that though their minds were free and willing, yet their bodies bowed under the*

weight of the same, and became decrepit in their early youth, the vigour of nature being consumed in the very bud as it were. But that which was more lamentable, and of all sorrows most heavy to be borne, was that many of their children, by these occasions and the great licentiousness of youth in that country and the manifold temptations of the place, were drawn away by evil examples into extravagant and dangerous courses, getting the reins off their necks and departing from their parents.

This is the story of that time.

In 1616, two years after this story, William Brewster set up his own printing firm in the Stink Alley house. In 1619, he had printed and sent to Scotland, in the false bottoms of French wine barrels, a tract critical of the king, called *Perth Assembly*. Because of it, English bailiffs raided Stink Alley and took all his printing equipment. Though they kept looking, the king's agents never captured him.

In 1620, Brewster, using a false name, sailed with his wife, Mary, and sons Love and Wrestling, along with sixty-four others of the Leiden congregation, from Delfshaven, Holland, to Southampton, England. It was the first leg of a trip that would take them to America on a ship named the *Mayflower*. Jonathan Brewster joined them in their home in the New World in 1621. Fear and Patience came in 1623.

Rembrandt Harmensz van Rijn finished Leiden Latin School at age thirteen and was registered by his father at the University of Leiden. He did not attend. Instead, he apprenticed with a local painter, Jacob van Swanenburgh. He set up his own studio in Leiden, then moved to Amsterdam, where he became one of the most famous artists in the world. He had a fine collection of seashells. Today, everybody calls him by just one name, Rembrandt. Nobody laughs at it.

Lizzy Tinker is a fictional character. But here's what I think happened to her. In 1619, when she was seventeen years old, she married Jan, the baker's son. She became known throughout Leiden for her *poffertjes*, little yeast-dough pancakes, which she grilled in their tidy street stall and served hot with butter and a sprinkling of sugar. All three of their daughters learned, at an early age, to ride, but never too high, the wings of a windmill.